FUR
AND
FEATHERS

GEORGE MURRAY

GEORGE MURRAY
PUBLICATIONS

FUR AND FEATHERS
(Living in the Past)

Is the intellectual property of the author
GEORGE MURRAY
All rights reserved 2014 © George Murray

Cover design, typesetting and logo design by
PAULA HÖRLING-MOSES
www.macmoses.net

Cover photos by
www.shutterstock.com

Printed in the United Kingdom by
LIGHTNING SOURCE UK LTD
Milton Keynes

Published by
GEORGE MURRAY PUBLICATIONS
Edinburgh
July 2016

ISBN 978-0-9927385-7-0

PROLOGUE

The Reformation was an event occurring throughout Europe and each country had its own peculiar and troubling circumstances as a result.

There were earlier schisms but the origins of the Reformation are normally recognised as the protest and criticism broadcast by the German priest Martin Luther who rebelled against the Church of Rome with his Ninety-five Theses in 1517. His protestations continued for four years during which time others had stood up to voice strong objections to the sale by the Roman Catholic Church of indulgences and offices and other seemingly corrupt practices. In Switzerland Huldrych Zwingli, a preacher and scholar, began his own movement in 1518 voicing similar objections but not truly reflecting Luther's reasoning. Martin Luther was excommunicated and the Reformation itself was condemned by the Pope. John Calvin took up the cause of the Reformation and instigated interest in central Europe. He undertook the task of raising the 'fallen city' of Geneva and drew others to him there, including the Scottish preacher, John Knox.

The spreading of the new faith was greatly assisted by the invention, in 1517, of the Gutenberg Press. Leaflets and booklets could be dispersed in thousands, carrying explanations and encouragement for the Reformation, from the presses under production in Mayence on the Rhine (now Mainz). Many accepted the revised views and growing divisions brought conflict and civil war. France demonstrated how much conflict was possible by swaying from an initially huge Protestant support to a heavy Roman Catholic backlash and the slaughter of tens of thousands of Huguenots (Protestants). All this before Henry IV's Edict of Nantes in 1598 called for tolerance of the Huguenots. French Protestantism declined over the following years. England had observed the French position and remained in confusion for a time after the death of Henry VIII who had declared himself head of the Church of England, independent of the Church of Rome. Elizabeth I presided over a country where the popular view was spread between extreme Calvinism and Roman Catholicism. She offered the uneasy compromise of Episcopacy where homages were mixed in their format and application by the church and many of the features of Roman Catholicism remained.

In Scotland the Reformation Parliament repudiated the Church of Rome and the Papacy with the Papal Jurisdiction Act 1560. The popular faith in Scotland was in accord with Luther and Calvin. The Church of Scotland had heard through John Knox of the spiritual need to answer only to God through his son, Jesus Christ. The Pope was not only regarded as unnecessary but some held him to be the anti-Christ. On 28th February 1638 the National Covenant was signed in Greyfriars Churchyard in Edinburgh and the Covenanters movement spread with fervour. It influenced the Puritan movement in England and the Puritans, with their sailing to the new world, spread the word to America. Scotland was now a Protestant country with an absentee Catholic queen, Mary, also Queen of France. There were Catholic sympathisers for Mary in Scotland but her reign would never be a happy one.

In the following century the Scots had watched the English fight out their differences in a civil war that pitched Oliver Cromwell against Charles I. Charles was beheaded and Cromwell ruled until his own death. Against the Stuarts, Cromwell had something akin to an ally in the Covenanters, but neither he nor Charles II, who returned from exile after Cromwell's death, could encourage the Scots to accept Episcopacy. The Church of Scotland felt so strongly opposed to the English church format, which they regarded as near to Roman Catholicism that they openly rebelled.

The Covenanters became victims of Charles II's determination to force episcopacy on Scotland. Presbyterian ministers were forced out of their churches to be replaced by prelates. These prelates were frustrated to find that their churches, normally packed for

Presbyterian services, could only attract a handful of parishioners to Episcopalian services. At the close of each service armed guards would take a note of the names and addresses of those who had attended. Those who were absent were deemed to be non-conformists and laws were passed to outlaw them.

The genuine preaching to the Presbyterian flock continued. It would take place in secluded rural, or secret, unheralded locations despite the enormous mortal danger invited by those forming these covert congregations, known as 'conventicles'.

All of this is a matter of history, little known outside Scotland, but it requires to be understood by those reading this novel. Readers should also be aware that a bhalaich is a friendly and agreeable Gaelic term by which to address a young man.

There are people who live in the past to the extent that they feel an empathy with forefathers from centuries before. I recall a Sunday school teacher in the 1960's relating how he and his wife had been to Glencoe on holiday. They had called at a cottage offering 'Bed and Breakfast'. Before confirming any availability the old lady of the house asked them what their name was. 'Mackinder' was the reply. 'Then I have a room for ye' was the reply. Mr Mackinder asked her why she had wanted their name and she had replied, 'If ye were a Campbell ye wouldnae be setting foot in my house'. Her own name was Macdonald.

It has to be said that such a stance would not necessarily have been taken by every Macdonald; my old friend Malcolm Macdonald Campbell can vouch for that. (His mother was a Macdonald). Those Scots, with memories that belie their years, are not normally too offensive to others, but there can be exceptions. In an already warped or unbalanced mind the notions of past misdeeds and the call for vengeance can be offensive and even dangerous to others.

With that in mind, I imagine you might be prepared for the reading of this story.

*"Vengeance is mine;
I will repay,
saith the Lord."*

ROMANS 12:19

ONE

The Lanarkshire moors of Scotland were seldom comfortable or warm, especially in the evening, winter or summer. Yet on an evening in 1682 a surprisingly large congregation had gathered in a shallow hollow to listen intently to a fervent preacher of the word of God. Around the group at some distance, armed men were stationed to look outwards across the moor. They watched and listened for any warning of approaching dragoons, for the brand of religion being practised was by then considered to be treason.

For almost half a century the supplicants, or covenanters, of the Church of Scotland had held robustly to their Presbyterian beliefs, resisting the attempts of the Roman Catholic Church, or the Anglican Church, to regain a controlling influence in Scotland. For generations the covenanters had necessarily resisted by civil warfare. A resistance in which they had enjoyed a measure of success.

In November 1666, the Rev. John Guthrie of Tarbolton, Ayrshire and 1,000 Galloway covenanters had entered the burgh town of Lanark and declared their support for the

National Covenant. They were joined by locals of the same inclination and all set off for Edinburgh. They were defeated in battle at Rullion Green, outside the city. Covenanters would never lack fervour but often lacked superior numbers and in matters of state, they had no say at all.

Following the execution of the Marquis of Argyll for treason and the Cromwell victory at Dunbar, James Sharp had been appointed Archbishop of St Andrews and primate for Scotland. Those ministers who did not recognise the authority of the bishops under the resumption of the High Commission were removed from office or had their livelihoods removed from beneath them. The return of Episcopacy was being forcibly imposed. Three hundred ministers of the Church of Scotland had been ousted from their positions to be replaced by Anglican curates. This had infuriated the covenanters and in 1679 they had been successful in assassinating James Sharp.

In 1680 a brave covenanter called Richard Cameron had ridden into the village of Sanquhar in Dumfriesshire accompanied by his brother and others. After a prayer at the village cross, he nailed a proclamation of defiance to the cross, a proclamation later known as The Declaration of Sanquhar. This made him a wanted man with a price of 5,000 Scots merks on his head. A month later, on the 22nd of July 1680, at Aird's Moss, he and his small band were attacked by a far superior number of horsemen. Richard Cameron had only time for a short prayer that he repeated twice, "Lord, spare the green and take the ripe." This was a reference to the depth of faith of his companions, not their age. He had died that day with seven others but there were survivors. Richard Cameron's head and hands were cut off and taken to Edinburgh. He was only 32 years of age. The example set by Cameron came to typify the stance of the covenanters who could be stopped only by death. They placed less earthly value on life than other men and saw death as a reward and recognition. They famously prayed while they fought. None ever yielded, in battle or in belief, and that made the government determined to eradicate them.

In January 1682, the covenanting army had returned to Lanark under James Renwick and a band of sixty men. Here, at the town cross, they read out the Declaration of Lanark, before defacing the cross with hammers. They declared allegiance to the earlier Declarations of Rutherglen and Sanquhar and repudiated the current laws of Charles II. For their support of the Covenant, four Lanark men were executed and others found their land and possessions forfeit to the Crown. Those not present at their homes were declared outlaws. The burgh council was fined 6,000 Scots merks for being tardy in dealing with the apprehension of the local covenanters.

In a period of reformation in Britain and Europe the success of the Scottish covenanters had risen and fallen with the changing attitudes and personalities of the monarch.

Now, later in 1682, the reigning monarch was still Charles II, the man who had once supported the covenant and accepted the doctrine of the General Assembly of the Church of Scotland. That had been his stance prior to his coronation at Scone, but now that he was king, he renounced Presbyterianism vehemently.

The dragoons threatening the conventicle on the moor that evening had the authority to carry out capital execution on the spot and without trial. To demonstrate the strength of Episcopalian objection to the covenanters, the bodies of those executed would not be buried in any decent fashion. Any attempt to bury a covenanter in a kirk churchyard was an offence that also carried a death penalty for those involved. To dishonour the deceased covenanters further, the bodies were often subjected to hanging or beheading after death. Such measures were designed to instil fear and disgrace in order to restore 'the divine right of kings', the long-held claim of the Stuart kings under the uncritical auspices of the Catholic church. To the minds of the covenanters this was heresy and erastianism.

In the congregation, an elderly Gabriel Ramsay listened to the zealous sermon. The preacher knew the danger they were all in and had chosen a text from Paul's letter to the Philippians, 'For me to live is Christ, to die is gain'. The unbending belief of the covenanter was to use life as an opportunity to live as devotedly as Christ lived. From that life and faith would come a gainful death. He was reminding all present of the need to stay strong and support the sacrifices of those who had lost their lives in the various civil conflicts since 1640 when the covenant, signed in 1638, had been adopted by the Scottish Parliament. The depth of support for a Presbyterian Scotland had been made clear at the time by the actions of Jenny Geddes, a female member of a congregation at St. Giles Cathedral, Edinburgh. When the Scottish prelate had attempted to introduce the revised Book of Common Prayer as a replacement for John Knox's Book of Discipline, she had allegedly called out "You'll no be saying ony mass in my lug (ear)". On shouting this she had famously thrown her stool at the Archbishop. The rest of the congregation had followed suit with anything that came to hand.

While the Covenanters had remained steadfast, the political situation had shifted.

This had long made conventicles, such as the one being attended on that evening in 1682, a capital offence for all present. It had taken real courage to gather on the moors, miles from their homes, but that did not mean that each person present did not have a genuine fear for their safety.

Gabriel Ramsay occasionally looked to his left where his son Daniel was on sentry duty. Daniel had a fine young wife called Martha and three small children, all girls. Grandfather Gabriel had much to fear. Off to his right a cry went up, "Dragoons".

The sound of hoof-beats had been muffled by the heather and the soldiers were already close. Daniel Ramsay ran to his father and bent a clutching arm around the old man, ushering him off towards a small bluff where they could hide. Successful concealment or fast feet was the only defence against the dragoons for the soldiers could never tell how many persons had first formed the scattering conventicle.

The two men lay beneath an overhang of ferns and heather, listening to the screams of women and groans of the men, as the pistols and swords of the soldiers took its terrible toll of the trapped worshippers. The preacher was being dragged off for a show trial before his inevitable sentence of death. The voice of the dragoon captain could be heard above the others. The capture of such a notable preacher would be 'a feather in his cap' and he was a man who rejoiced in bringing death to the covenanters.

"That's Ratline." Gabriel whispered to his son. Young Daniel simply nodded.

The sounds of single horses moving out from the centre of activity was now the threat. The horses were moving slowly as their riders twisted about in their saddles to examine the surrounding area for escapees. Almost without any sound at all, a grey mare rounded the bluff and stopped directly in front of the two Ramsay men. The trapped covenanters looked up into the sneering face of the dragoon captain.

"Well, Gabriel Ramsay. I think I shall soon lay claim to that pitiful mill of yours."

Daniel Ramsay attempted to stand up in protest but Lynus Ratline simply lifted his pistol and shot the young man between the eyes, killing him instantly.

For a moment Gabriel looked in shock at his son's body. The old man had seen violent death so often before but the reality of this death went deeper. He turned towards Ratline in rage, slowly rising to his feet as he spoke.

"You have murdered my son, Ratline, killed my seed, so that none can reclaim my mill. But I shall be avenged." Gabriel Ramsay closed his eyes but continued to point his Bible towards the soldier. "Almighty God avenge me and wipe that sneer from the face of this brute of a man. Cause his seed to suffer extinction." the old man imprecated with passion as he thrust his Bible towards the captain, who now stared down with open eyes, more angry than triumphant.

"How dare you threaten me." was the response, as he moved his horse forward and brought his sword down forcibly into the skull of the old covenanter. Ratline jumped down from his horse and without checking if the men were dead, he hacked both heads from their bodies. He lifted the heads by their hair and climbed back into his saddle. The headless bodies were left where they lay with no obvious prospect of a proper burial. Ratline would use the heads of Gabriel and Daniel Ramsay to show that both had died and their possessions stood to be forfeited. In the case of Gabriel Ramsay's mill, the property would go directly to Ratline.

A few days later a group of villagers came to the death scene, armed with picks and spades. They worked in silence as they dug out graves for the remains left by the dragoons. Their children had been brought with them for safety reasons but the young ones were encouraged to play well away from the grave-digging.

One child, Elisabeth Thomson, walked around the small 'hills' she found nearby, busily talking to herself to describe the landscape she chose to see. Behind one of her small hills she found the decapitated corpses of Gabriel Ramsay and his son, Daniel. After a sharp intake of breath the girl moved slowly closer, her eyes staring at the sight.

Within feet of Gabriel Ramsay lay his Bible, an English language edition of the Geneva Bible, similar to the one her own father had. She lifted it and opened the book. Written on the fly-leaf in a scrawling script was the name 'Gabriel Ramsay an owner of the covenant and a servant of Jesus Christ'.

She closed the book and pressed it to her chest. "I will look after your Bible for you Mister Ramsay."

She then called aloud to her father that there were two more bodies behind the 'hill'.

Lynus Ratline sold the mill shortly thereafter, using the money to settle some of his gambling debt.

As the years of the seventeenth century rolled out towards the early years of the eighteenth, the Presbyterian

Church of Scotland survived with a greater tolerance of other faiths. King James VI Act of Indulgence of 1687 had beseeched a peace in which all were 'to serve God after their own way and manner'. This permitted the covenanters to survive despite their reluctance towards the established government.

In 1689, after the arrival of William of Orange and the consolidation of the Protestant reformation, the remaining covenanters were isolated from the government forces by their own strong Presbyterian faith but were formed into a regiment by the young Earl of Angus of the house of Douglas, in Lanarkshire. They came to be known as the Cameronians, in recognition of Richard Cameron. Their commander was Lieutenant-Colonel William Clelland, a talented leader of only 28 years of age having proved his worth at the Battle of Drumclog.

The government forces, still fighting a Stuart opposition, had been routed at the Battle of Killiecrankie that year and had fled in disarray. It was imperative from the government perspective to stop the Jacobite forces, loyal to the Catholic Stuarts, from marching further south. The Cameronians, an untried regiment, variously reported as being 800 to 1200 strong, were deployed to Dunkeld in Perthshire to stop the Jacobites. The only fortified part of Dunkeld was the walled curtilage of the cathedral and it was within these walls that William Clelland took station.

On 21st August 1689, facing an opposition of 5000 men, the Cameronians fought all day until nightfall.

Running low on ammunition, they stripped lead from the cathedral roof and created a fresh supply of musket balls. The Jacobites retreated and returned north.

Presbyterian Scotland would continue to denounce the previous government's treatment of covenanters as a disgrace to the country and the early years of the eighteenth century saw the erection of tombstones and memorial stones to honour the martyrs of the covenanting struggle. The atmosphere had changed significantly and many of these memorials were to be found within church graveyards, something unthinkable for much of the seventeenth century.

Out on the moor, at the site of the Ramsays' last conventicle, a large stone, split into two and opened like a book, had been sunk into the peaty soil. On the flat inner surfaces of each half were carved the names of those who had died that night at the hands of Ratline's dragoons.

In the summer of 1700, when Elisabeth Thomson had reached the age of twenty-four years, she married a fine young man named Daniel Sorbie. Her husband was a carpenter who worked in a rural area close to the village of Lesmahagow, Lanarkshire. While they continued in the Presbyterian faith of their parents, the couple were given to using the recently issued King James Bible. Determined to keep her promise to old Gabriel Ramsay, Elisabeth Sorbie asked her husband to make her a small box in which to keep the Geneva Bible from the moor. In due course she would pass it on to her own children.

Mining had become a major industry in the Scottish lowlands in the eighteenth century and coal fuel was the main driving force for an economy increasingly reliant on heavy manufacturing. Tin was also mined sufficiently to meet market demands. The demands from mining and quarrying grew throughout that century and into the next.

In 1808 houses were built by mining companies at Wilsontown, Lanarkshire, to accommodate their miners. These houses took the form of long terraces of single storeyed dwellings where each family, regardless of size, was able to live for as long as the husband and his sons were employed by the mining company. Railways were built to convey the coal and other ores from the pits until the production ceased to be viable. The company would then move elsewhere.

In 1931 a major source of coal was opened near to the village of Forth and as work increased the miners transferred to the new pit. Smaller pits had become uneconomical and in 1936 the miners' rows at Wilsontown, near to Forth, were condemned and after 128 years of good service, Quality Row, Wilsontown was demolished. The miners from these houses had to find houses from which they could travel each day to Kingshill No.2, the large recently developed mine outside Forth.

The village of Forth had absorbed all the miners it could take and accommodation was only available at an ever-increasing distance from the mine.

So it was in 1938 that a group of eight miners, all resident on the north side of Carluke village, travelled eight miles each day to reach Kingshill No. 2. They cycled for the first four miles by road before leaving their bikes behind the farm wall alongside the road. To have continued by road would have meant a further sixteen miles but, by walking across the moor, the distance was shortened to four miles. They did this in all weathers and at all times of the year.

Through time they wore out a path through the heather and, even in snowstorms, they could find their way. The path took them past 'the Covenanters Stane', which was seen on each journey, some thirty yards from the path.

As the men were returning one evening in November, darkness was falling and they were bemoaning the fact that they could soon be finding things more difficult. As they were passing the 'Stane', they scarcely thought to look at it but one of their number glanced sideways and stopped in shock horror at what he saw. "Look." was all he could find to say.

The others did look and all stood rooted to the spot as they saw two men standing beside the two halves of the same stone. From their clothing, these figures were not miners, nor even present day citizens. The two bodies seemed to be composed of smoke rather than flesh and blood. They had no colour at all and to make matters worse, both were without heads.

After staring at these apparitions for several moments, the miners began to move towards them. The figures dissolved out of sight. The miners went to the memorial stone and remarked among themselves on what they had just witnessed. They also agreed that the temperature had dropped considerably.

The men continued to use the path and paid attention to 'the stane' each time they passed, but they never experienced a repetition of this spiritual event. Their story became part of local folk lore. Such stories were not uncommon. Children exploring the moor were forever finding old musket balls or rusty weapons, keeping afloat the stories from local history, stories told in the warmth of coal fires.

The Cameronians continued to serve as a regiment of the British army.

In 1872 the 3rd Battalion of the Lanark Rifle Volunteers (Cameronians) formed a football team called Third Lanark. This team played in the top Scottish leagues until 1967.

The Cameronians themselves, as a Scottish regiment, were disbanded in 1968 at Douglas, Lanarkshire.

Three centuries after the 'killing times' of the covenanters, the struggles had been largely forgotten, despite the loss of eighteen thousand lives. If history lessons broached on the subject of the covenanters at all, it would simply be to mention the battles at Aird's Moss and Bothwell Brig. Scottish history was serialised warfare and brutality. The covenanters' time was simply one more episode.

TWO

In 1966 Karen Thomson was a happy fifteen years old schoolgirl attending Stonehouse Junior Secondary School at Townhead, Stonehouse, Lanarkshire. She was an intelligent girl with aspirations of becoming a fine school teacher someday, just like Miss Kit Small, one of her present teachers and a great role model to Karen, despite being forty-five years older. At the end of this school year Karen hoped to move to Hamilton Academy and thereafter to Jordanhill College in Glasgow.

In the meantime she spent her leisure hours in the company of her friend and cousin, Jennifer Paterson. The difference in the nature of the girls seemed to bond them firmly as ideal companions. Jennifer would encourage Karen to attend the Saturday matinee at the cinema or to go with her to the fairground whenever the 'shows' were in town. Karen, for her part, was the reason for Jennifer's membership of the Girl Guides and the pair's regular summer camps. Jennifer's mother was a sister to Karen's father and had been a Thomson before marrying. In Mrs Paterson's possession was an old Bible handed down through generations of the Thomson family with nothing known about it, other than its alleged origins in covenanting times.

On most days the girls could be found together in Stonehouse, just idly watching the activities of others and taking note of anything or anyone unusual.

One Saturday morning they noticed a woman who could certainly be described as 'strange'. The woman looked as if she should be old but was possibly younger than her appearance suggested. Her long black hair was neither clean nor combed; her posture was slightly stooped as if she carried an unseen burden on her shoulders; her long black dress with a ragged hem beneath an unbuttoned cardigan; all conspired to age her. The woman's sprightly movements, however, belied this impression of age, as she darted from one pedestrian to another with a question or an offer that nobody seemed keen to take up.

"That's the Galloway witch," Jennifer told Karen. "She has been here before."

"She looks like someone who's been everywhere before." Karen replied, smiling to herself at the strange figure under discussion. "What does she do?"

"She claims to tell fortunes." Jennifer said. "My mother always says to avoid these people."

"What harm can she do?" Karen wondered aloud.

The girls stood and watched the progress of the strange woman and did not shy away as she drew closer. Suddenly the woman darted towards them.

"Want to know your fortunes, girls? I can tell you how life will turn out for ye. I have the gift, you see."

Now that the girls could see her piercing bright eyes they knew that this woman was not at all elderly.

"You want money and we don't have any." Jennifer said positively.

The woman's eyes switched to and fro from one girl to the other.

"Suppose you are a bit young," she conceded. How about sixpence? Can you come up with sixpence?"

"Is that for both of us?" Karen asked, confirming the stranger's suspicion of which girl might have some money.

"My word, you are a shrewd one. What's your name little girl?"

"Karen Thomson"

"A good covenanter's name that." the woman remarked turning to Jennifer. "And what is your name girl?"

"Jennifer Paterson"

"Are you covenanting stock?"

"My mother has a covenanter's Bible." Jennifer replied, suspecting that her answer would please the old woman.

"That would be the grocer's wife." the woman thought aloud.

"Will you take sixpence?" Karen reminded her.

"Yes, luvvie. If that's what ye have then that's what it'll be. Give it here."

Karen produced the sixpence that had been intended for the purchase of a chocolate bar. The woman took it and dropped it into the pocket of her old cardigan before turning again to Jennifer.

"Let's see your hand, lass." she said kindly enough, lifting Jennifer's open hand onto her own. "Ah, look now, you have a long life ahead. I see you working with foodstuffs, maybe in a shop. You will marry too and have two children, both girls. I don't find anything evil up ahead for you."

She released Jennifer's hand and lifted Karen's hand in the same way. She gasped as she looked down into Karen's palm.

"Oh lass, I see tragedy here. You will live through the tragedy but it will scar you deep. You will marry unwisely and .." she stopped. "You seem to love children so I will not continue. You will be happy one day, never fear."

At that the woman sped away, leaving the two friends to look at each other in bewilderment.

"What do you make of that?" Jennifer asked.

Karen did not wish to support her friend's tendency towards superstition.

"I think that was pretty poor for sixpence. I would rather have a cake of chocolate any day."

Life continued for Jennifer and Karen who soon forgot all about the fortune-teller and her forecast of tragedy.

On leaving school, Karen pursued her career and attended college. Jennifer simply took a greater part in the family business.

When Jennifer began work in her parents' grocery business she had no thought of the woman's prediction. She married and had two children, both girls.

The Paterson's grocery business followed the style of independent grocers in Lanarkshire for years. Customers were treated as personal friends and regular customers placed regular orders for the grocer to deliver, normally each week. The younger Jennifer had worked in her father's shop 'making up' each order for delivery, but now that she was older, able to drive and with both girls at school, it was she who took the large brown cardboard bags on a delivery round.

The manse was a regular call on her route and it sat in a splendid country setting. Jennifer always enjoyed calling there and often stayed long enough to enjoy home-made scones and tea provided by the minister's wife.

Her mother had informed the minister in conversation of the Bible in her possession and he had expressed an interest in seeing the book. For that reason Mrs Paterson had given the box containing the old Bible to Jennifer one Thursday night, knowing that she would be visiting the manse with groceries the following day.

On Friday afternoon Jennifer stopped her car in the lane leading past the manse and took from the back seat of her car, the sack of groceries and the wooden box. As she turned to carry them to the large white cottage, a young man with dirty hair ran from the bushes nearby and pushed her to the ground. He then struck her on the face and lifted the bag of groceries and the wooden box. A dazed and bleeding Jennifer was aware of him running back into the bushes that he had come from but she never saw him again. She went to the manse and the minister's wife called the police before attending to Jennifer's bleeding nose.

Jennifer took greater care on her delivery round after that incident but there were no further attacks of that kind. Her assailant was not traced.

Karen Thomson succeeded at college and became a primary school teacher, one year after the retirement of her hero and role model. She had been teaching for three years when she met an attractive young insurance agent with an Australian accent and ambitious hopes for his future.

Fraser was so different from Karen and his extrovert personality shocked her occasionally but just like Jennifer Paterson had once been, his different attitudes brought him closer to Karen. He would never expect or accept 'no' for an answer. Karen preferred to lead a life tolerant of everyone and everything, never allowing any risk to materialise or argument to develop. This tended to make their relationship one-sided with Fraser's views always dominant. For that reason Karen, with parental advice, took her time to allow the true picture of Fraser to appear. Time made little difference to their personalities but they somehow compromised sufficiently to remain together.

It was two years later, in 1977, that Karen married Fraser, now an area manager for the whole of Scotland. It was a quiet church ceremony, confined to Karen's closest relatives. Fraser had no relatives or friends to call on but seemed satisfied with the deference being shown by size of the company. As the couple left the church there was no more than a handful of kind neighbours across the street to cheer and shout their good wishes. Karen was happy to recognise those present until her eyes fell on someone from several years before. The middle-aged woman who had once offered to tell young Karen her fortune for sixpence stood apart from the others and smirked at the newly-wed couple in a way that worried Karen.

Karen had no worries over income or Fraser's commitment to her and his work, but his driving was a genuine concern. She had been afraid of his driving each time she had been his passenger and she was not alone in her fear.

Fraser's subordinate colleagues in the insurance group refused to accompany him on business trips unless they were doing the driving. Fraser was fast and proud of it, always seeking to impress with fast driving that was anything but impressive. Karen was unaware of it, but all colleagues of the company had drawn up a document, to be agreed by the company directors, that on no account could any of them be required to sit as a passenger in the vehicle being driven by Fraser. The company had agreed. Fraser would always be on his own while driving, even Karen chose to provide her own transport.

While the young schoolteacher was normally driving her small new car around locally to shops and other essential destinations, Fraser had responsibility for every region in Scotland and gave little consideration to safe speed, strange roads and adverse weather.

The results of such failings were familiar to Police Constable Andrew Fleming who was enjoying life with his young wife and family in the idyllic splendour of the West Highlands. All too often a single occupant vehicle would be travelling at excessive speed on the main roads where long straight sections of road seemed to encourage the idea. Nature had not permitted for all sections of road to be created straight and level, however. The vast openness gave the driver a false impression of his speed and before he could react safely, some sudden change in the road would catch him or her out and tragedy would result. It was a familiar and predictable pattern.

An example of this had happened that week at the end of August 1979. A young man from the lowlands had been rushing north on business for an insurance company. He had promised his young wife that he would be home by evening despite having no prior knowledge of the journey ahead of him. In the late forenoon, he was heading for Fort William on a straight stretch of road when his attention was drawn to the sheltered snow patches high on the mountains. The sky was blue and flying close to the road was a buzzard that dived down from the blue background to pounce on some unseen prey in the heather. The driver did not appreciate the time he had spent looking at this and when he looked back towards the road ahead, he found himself heading at speed towards the front of a large lorry with the name 'Cameron' across the cab. He swerved violently away to avoid the lorry but left the road and was thrown through the air into a large sunken rock.

His speed at the time of impact could only be guessed at by the enquiring traffic police officers, but it had been sufficiently great as to crush his car back to the driver's seat. The impact had not dislodged the rock, but had cracked it into two halves. The young man had died at the scene from head injuries.

In her Lanarkshire village home, Karen heard the distinct knock on the door. Most callers would use the doorbell, but this was a knock with bare knuckles and it made her feel wary. She opened the door to find a tall, heavily built policeman. She did not know this man by name but he was the local bobby. His expression was sombre.

"You are Mrs Karen Ratline, I believe?" he said softly.

"I am." Karen replied equally softly. She could feel the blood drain from her face as she sensed the day she had dreaded for so long.

"Then I am extremely sorry to say that your husband

has been involved in a road accident on the road to Fort William. He was driving his Mercedes."

The officer got no further for Karen had supposed the rest of what he had to say and the policeman had to swoop forward to catch her as she fainted. He carried her into the house and laid her on her couch before summoning an ambulance by radio. In a small village a resident's life is not so secret from others and the local doctor was also summoned by telephone. The police officer knew that Karen Ratline, who had just lost her husband to a road accident, was seven months pregnant with their first child.

Road traffic accidents, particularly serious ones, were part of a tragic but routine diet as far as Fleming was concerned. He needed something different to occupy his mind.

His friendship with fishermen and others with boats had made him interested in having a boat of his own. His friend Calum had a fast sixteen footer with an outboard engine and another friend, Donald, had a beautiful yacht. Andrew Fleming could never hope to match these craft but he kept an eye open for anything to suit a low budget.

Another friend, called Douglas, had heard of Fleming's wish to own a boat and offered him a hull and an inboard engine. The cost was low and, if Fleming was prepared to do the work, the boat could be completed without too much further cost. Fleming agreed.

It took six months and more money than Fleming had intended spending, but the boat finally became seaworthy. He bought lifejackets and flares from trusted sources and a radio from the mountain rescue team. Now 'The Marlin' could take to sea.

Initially he went out alone, or in the company of someone who could teach him seamanship. The family would have to wait until he had confidence before they could expect any trips to shoreline picnic spots. In the meantime, he took his boat around the inshore coasts, occasionally rod fishing but always looking for suitable places to do some creel fishing.

Christmas 1979, was not the festive event it should have been for Karen Ratline. Her baby son had been born in October and had been named Callum Fraser Ratline. Fraser had chosen 'Callum' as the name for his son, if it was to be a boy. Even in death, Fraser got his way, but Karen for once, fully agreed. It had seemed to her that the whole village had turned out to support her at Fraser's funeral in the local church. He had not been popular with everyone locally, something Karen had never found a reason for, but she had been aware of it.

Her parents invited her for Christmas but Karen was all too conscious of the missing figure at the dinner table. Baby Callum could not be expected to understand the occasion. A child's first Christmas was something that close relatives enjoyed and were appreciative of, at least those who were present.

The birth of Callum had been a natural birth despite the circumstances and Karen was on maternity leave, a respite that no-one could begrudge her. The children at school had brought tears to her eyes with considerate presents purchased by parents who felt her sorrow. Their thoughtfulness helped to lift Karen's spirit and she resolved to make life good for little Callum.

Fraser had always forced her to accompany him at New Year as he went 'first-footing' at the homes of those few rougher types that he knew in the village. Of course it had been contrary to the quiet-natured Karen but she had done what her husband wanted and now she warmed to the thought of missing that particular tradition. She had no wish to drink and socialise this New Year.

In the month of February the weather in Lanarkshire was clear and healthy. Clear skies meant overnight frost and the morning would pull a reluctant sun above the skyline to brighten the outlook. It was not warm, but at this time of year it was as good as it got. Karen wrapped little Callum up in warm woollen clothing and blankets before taking him in his pram to the graveyard beyond the church. She had been notified by the Funeral Directors that Fraser's headstone was now in place and she was keen to see it.

An old bent woman watched her from a distance but when Karen entered the graveyard she found the place deserted. The low sun was causing long shadows across grass that was green where the sunlight fell and white everywhere else. Her Fraser's headstone stood out from the rest. It was in new black marble with gold lettering. She would have lifted Callum to see it but he was asleep. She parked his pram on the opposite side of the path in front of a tall memorial stone to someone called 'Cameron' and let the sun's rays fall on him.

She went to the new stone and read it over and over. Her husband had been a wild and difficult man but she had loved him. With all his faults she had consciously made the marriage decision for herself. She had surprised herself, Karen Thomson making major decisions for herself without consultation with parents, or anyone else. She had wanted Fraser and in his own way, he had wanted her. Now he was as close as he would ever be again. She had chosen his headstone too. She bent towards the stone and wept.

Behind her she was conscious of a breaking sound and a loud thump. The memorial stone to 'Cameron' rose to a point on which a stone orb had formed a top. A large round stone, some 15 inches in diameter, had just dislodged itself from the point above her head and fallen directly into her baby's pram.

She screamed loudly and frantically clawed at the heavy stone, finding strength she would not normally possess, to roll the orb out of the pram and onto the path. She looked at Callum and felt weak. She lifted him and begged him to cry but the child remained silent and eerily limp. She wept into the warm, soft blanket surrounding her son but still felt compelled to look in the direction of the cemetery gate. The same bent woman was standing there, looking at Karen, but when Karen looked back, the woman withdrew. It had been that fortune-teller woman again. Karen was sure of it.

Within minutes others came. She fought desperately to forget that day even as it was happening. She would later recall vaguely the ambulance men and that same village policeman, the doctor and some lady who promised to contact Karen's mum. It was all too much.

On a warm, dry March day of that year Fleming idly steered his boat around some rocky points well away from any habitation or public roads. Most of the shoreline looked impenetrable but he did find a small cove with a gradual beach of shingle. His twenty-foot boat would not be able to reach the shore, so he threw his plough anchor over the side and lowered the inflatable dinghy from the cabin roof. With very little effort he was able to row ashore and tie off the dinghy to some roots at the back of the beach.

He could already hear a strange noise across the point, beyond the bushes and trees. He made his way through the undergrowth and bracken until he could see the cause of the noise.

A woman of at least fifty years of age was sitting

cross-legged beside a wood fire, mumbling incoherently into the flames. She had long dark grey hair that had not seen a comb or brush in years and, like her complexion, appeared darker, due to smoke, dirt and a lack of washing. Her clothes had an ever-present look and were certainly not clean. She seemed to suit her present surroundings and Fleming looked around for any kind of habitation, but saw none. The water's edge on her side of the headland had no boats of any description and yet it was hard to imagine any other method of coming and going to this place on a regular basis. How did she get by?

The woman rose slowly from the ground, her eyes still fixed on the fire and she began to slowly move around the fire. Her mumbling became louder and was now more like a chant. Soon her voice was loud enough for Fleming to hear what she was saying.

"From the covenanter's grave, a stane; did fall and kill the bonnie wean."

This line was being repeatedly chanted and the voice grew stronger as the old woman seemed to grow more agitated and her movement became a skip. She suddenly stopped as if her muscles had spontaneously contracted. She closed her wide staring eyes and let out a loud piercing scream as if a terrible pain had struck her. The scream stopped and she slumped to the ground. Fleming remained still and wondered at this performance. Somehow he realised that the woman was not in any physical trouble. Had this charade been done just for his benefit? He had felt sure that she had never known of his presence, but was he wrong?

The woman stirred and raised a hand to her head. Her other hand pushed her body up to a sitting position. She now looked like someone awakening from a sleep. Fleming turned and slipped away. He crept back the way he had come trying to make as little noise as possible. When he reached his inflatable dinghy he stared in disbelief. The inflated perimeter was divided into zones internally so that any leaking of air would not affect the whole hull. The starboard front zone was deflated and Fleming could easily see why. The top surface had been punctured to leave a half-inch slit. It looked like a puncture made by a small knife blade but the place was deserted. Or was it? His eyes scanned the trees and bushes nearest to him and he listened intently. He walked beyond the shingle and looked for any indication of some person having been there. He found nothing.

The dinghy would not float back to The Marlin if he was on board. He stripped down to his underwear and placed the oars and his clothing in the rear port-side corner, hoping to raise the deflated starboard side. He crept into the cold water with the painter between his teeth and over his shoulder. He swam out to The Marlin and lifted the dinghy on board. With a final stare back along the treeline, he started the diesel engine and left the cove. Could a sea-bird have caused the puncture? Fleming could picture a bird dropping a mussel from height to break the shell, but shook his head. The Zodiac dinghy was tough and would not succumb to anything like that.

The next day, on his return to duty, Fleming asked among his colleagues if anyone knew the strange female hermit he had seen. The only person with a positive answer was the Chief Inspector. Stewart Mackellar could recall such a woman from years before.

"She was more inclined in her younger days to come into the town and beg for food. She would pretend to tell fortunes for ten shillings and that sort of thing. She usually had a baby with her. Some cynical people suggested that the child was being used for sympathy purposes but nobody ever knew who she really was. Local folks called her the 'Galloway Witch' and I guessed she must have come from Galloway but she disappeared after a while. It seemed most likely that she had moved on." Mackellar remembered.

"Where did she live?" Fleming asked.

"Nobody really knew." Mackellar replied. "I was just a young constable at that time and the woman was more of an oddity than a troublemaker, so we never had cause to take her in. The local talk was that she lived in a cave but then it would be, she looked for all the world like someone who lived in a cave. She was anything but clean. Is that the kind of person you saw?"

"Yes." Fleming answered. "Allowing for the passing of years, it could well be her. She had a camp fire but if there was a cave, I never saw it."

That seemed to be the end of the conversation but as Fleming turned to go, he stopped and looked back at Mackellar.

"This fortune-telling, was she any good at it?"

Mackellar laughed.

"How the hell would I know?"

"Right enough, sir. You are not the type to part with ten bob."

The summer season of 1982 had started slowly but with the milder weather and for some, sheer force of habit, the visitors began to arrive in decent numbers. During the day the shops on Main Street were busy with customers of different nationalities, skin colour and accents. In the evenings the hotels and restaurants were alive with custom and Corran Bay looked more like a holiday resort. The town was at its capacity during the overlap of Scottish and English school breaks.

Gordon Cargill locked his Rover car near the town square and walked round to the offices of Cargill, Russell and Ridgeway to begin another day's work.

He had practised law in Corran Bay for over thirty years and never had the desire to live anywhere else. His wife Marjorie had passed away five years earlier and her death had removed a great deal of his personal satisfaction and motivation. His large detached house and garden on the coast road north of the town had always been on the excessively large side since his family of one boy, Donald, and one daughter, Marjorie, usually called Midge, had grown to maturity and flown to London and Jersey, respectively. That had been ten years earlier and although Gordon still welcomed each sunny day, like this one and the friendship of those he and Marjorie had come to know well, life was empty. The one abiding motivation for Gordon was his business. The law firm remained in good heart and his young partners of eight years, Cameron Russell and Robert Ridgeway, had proved themselves worthy of continuing the firm when Gordon would no longer be around.

The elderly lawyer was already in his seventies and might have retired before now had Marjorie lived to share matters with him, but he had clung to his work as one reaches to a lifebelt when struggling in troubled waters.

Quite recently, with his garden needing more attention than he had time to spare and his workload decreasing towards favoured clients the realities of his age were conspiring to force a return to his thoughts of retirement. These thoughts annoyed him as he climbed the stairs but when he entered the office to cheery calls of 'Good Morning, Mister Cargill' from his young secretarial staff, all such annoying notions were forgotten.

Robert Ridgeway, the younger of his two partners came to him with a delicate matter concerning local authority restrictions on a planning consent for a client. Gordon Cargill knew practically everyone in the council offices and was respected sufficiently to manage situations like this. He asked for the file and then placed the call. Five minutes later and the problem had gone away. Such moments as these brought back some of the old comfort and satisfaction. He was enjoying his day.

When his secretary called through to report that, 'Mrs Galloway and her son are in the front office, wishing to see you, Mr Cargill', Gordon knew immediately that his day had just developed a major downturn. This unhygienic pair were quite the last thing he needed. It was true that they were his responsibility as clients. He had set up Mrs Galloway's late husband's trust, in terms of his will, but that had been twenty years ago. Now the money had run out and he had no record of her current address by which to mail her a notification. He had written to her mother's address in Stonehouse. Perhaps word had finally reached her.

"All right, Mrs Scott, show them in." he replied with no hint of enthusiasm. This pair did not really qualify as 'favoured clients'.

Gordon Cargill gulped as the pair entered. The Galloways had never been clean and tidy but the years since he had last seen them had not been kind. The mother very poorly dressed in faded, dirty clothing. Her hair was matted and had not seen a brush or comb in years. Her sallow complexion and sagging skin made her appear years older than Cargill knew her to be. The skin and flesh around her face hung like melting wax and a dewlap had formed beneath her chin.

As shocking as the mother's appearance had become, it was her son who drew Cargill's attention. When the lawyer had last seen the son he had seen a babe in arms, now this small boy was tall and dark. His black hair was filthy and unkempt, his facial hair was neither clean-shaven nor full beard. The man, for he was now age enough to be called a man, wore dirty stained clothes and muddy sports shoes.

Gordon Cargill looked intently at the young man's eyes. They produced a blank but worrying stare. The lawyer sensed that he was not as well developed mentally as he was physically. This threatening demeanour might not be helpful when the subject of their visit was not going to please his mother.

"Did you receive my letter, Mrs Galloway?" Cargill asked, purposefully neglecting to invite the pair to sit.

"My mother told me about it. You are going to stop my money." Jessie Sorbie or Galloway said in an accusing voice.

"That is not what the letter said, Mrs Galloway." Cargill corrected. "What it said was that the funds of the trust had expired. In other words, Mrs Galloway, your late husband's trust fund has run out money and can no longer provide the payments you have been receiving."

"But he had eighteen thousand pounds, where has it gone?" the woman was stubborn in her determination to accuse rather than accept.

"The truth of that, is that it has gone to you, Mrs

Galloway, as it was intended. In fact, over the period of the trust you have received in excess of twenty-one thousand pounds, but the funds are now exhausted. There have been periods of growth during the term but unfortunately for yourself, the effect of inflation has meant that an annual payment of £1000 paid in monthly deposits to your own bank account is not as healthy an income as it was in your husband's lifetime. I dare say he expected you to be better provided for, but even he knew that the insurance pay-out would not last forever."

"If he was here now he would be sorting you lot out." the woman suggested. "He would see that I got my money."

"Yes, he probably would, Mrs Galloway, just as he always did, by going out and working for it. Do either of you work?"

"Do we look like we can work?" Jessie Galloway hissed defiantly. "We don't have a roof over our heads, never mind a place to work."

"Well, you may have to try." Cargill insisted. "This firm can no longer provide you money from a trust fund that is empty." As he spoke he lifted the internal telephone.

"Mrs Scott can you look out the copy letter sent to Mrs Galloway at the Stonehouse address and ask Robert to bring it in please?"

Mrs Scott had already brought out the file in expectation and a few moments later, Robert Ridgeway entered the office and placed the letter in front of Gordon. The older solicitor lifted and turned the letter so that Jessie Galloway could see it.

"Is this the letter you received at your mother's?" he asked.

"Don't know. Can't read without glasses." Jessie Sorbie replied sourly.

"Then I shall read it for you. It says what I have been telling you. The trust fund set up following the death of your husband in February 1962, in accordance with his will of eighth August 1959, has now exhausted the funds available. As a result of this you will no longer receive a monthly payment of £83.33. Your final payment, on 15th July 1982, will be for the sum of £62.43. No further payments will follow."

Cargill turned the letter and placed it in front of Jessie Galloway, handing her a pen.

"Please be so kind as to sign the bottom of the letter, Mrs Galloway. Just to show that you have seen it. My associate, Mr Ridgeway and I will state that the contents were read to you since you could not read it yourself."

Jessie Galloway drew her thin lips together in anger and stared at the document before lifting the pen that Cargill had offered her and threw it at him. The pen bounced off his shoulder.

"You're nothing but thieves, the lot of you. I'll see you in hell, Gordon Cargill." she raged as she turned and stormed out of the office. Her son, who had never opened his mouth, turned and followed her.

"Charming." commented Ridgeway.

"It could have been worse, Robert." Cargill remarked, recalling the menacing eyes of the son. "I'll dictate a note to Cathie for the bottom of this letter, explaining what took place. We can both sign to that effect. She has been informed and I don't see what else we can do. She has no address of her own apparently."

The traffic outside was noisy but Cargill felt obliged to open his office window and allow some fresh air to replace the odour left by his visitors. By the end of that working day Gordon Cargill had decided on how he wanted to proceed. He would work over the summer to allow other members of the firm to take their summer vacations before bowing out gracefully in the autumn. He informed his younger partners of his intentions and worked late, leaving the office last of all the staff, as usual.

As he drove around the square on his way home, Gordon saw the Galloway pair again. He gave an involuntary shiver as he passed them but they seemed not to have noticed him. Their attention was elsewhere, on a small white car with cheerful stickers, parked outside a block of recently built flats.

Andrew Fleming enjoyed the town of Corran Bay at all times of the year but during the school holidays he would take the family north to golden beaches and blue sea where only the locals knew of their existence. Fleming had been fortunate enough to make the acquaintance of people in Ullapool and their secrets were now his secrets.

While he was on holiday with Mary and the children he would find nothing but peace. The same was not true for those he had left behind in Corran Bay.

On a warm summer evening a young, mentally refreshed Karen Ratline was driving south towards Corran Bay and was well aware of the sea appearing now and then on her right side, the lowering sun was reflected on the water. Since she had moved into her flat in town she had driven on this road practically every evening.

Only three weeks had passed since she had taken possession of her keys to the flat and supervised the arrival of her possessions. She had dutifully reported her arrival and given her address to the local council. She had also registered with a doctor and the local dentist. These moments of contact had carried a sense of expectancy on the part of those she spoke to, almost as if they had known she was coming. Wherever she had gone during her three weeks she had the feeling of being noticed, even watched, by people she did not yet know.

When she found the place where the water came closest to the road, she parked her small car and walked through the reeds and grass towards the water's edge. She could feel the warmth of the sun but there was a fresh breeze coming off the sea and she considered the possibility of returning to this spot during the day with a picnic lunch, but in the evening there was never anyone else around.

She looked for a rock or something that might provide

a seat for her to sit. She found nothing immediately and forced her way through some whin bushes and rhododendrons. She almost fell over a man who was sitting in the grass with a fishing rod in his hand. The man grabbed her and pulled her down to the ground.

Two hours later, a local ambulance driver saw the parked car and stopped to check it out. It was difficult to imagine why anyone might want to park at that spot as darkness was falling. He saw some indication in the vehicle that the owner was probably female. A handbag lay on the passenger seat and pink dice hanging from the rear view mirror suggested a strange abandonment by a female owner. The ambulance driver walked into the grass and bushes behind the parked car and heard a low moaning sound. The noise led him to the half-naked body of a badly beaten woman.

He summoned assistance and the woman was removed to the hospital at Corran Bay. The hospital staff called the police as the young woman had been badly injured and sexually attacked. When the CID attended and spoke with her doctors it was evident that the victim had been raped and beaten into unconsciousness. Without the intervention of the ambulance driver, the woman would probably have succumbed to her injuries. Detective Sergeant Campbell would have to wait until the following day before any interview of the patient would be permissible. The doctor's opinion had just raised the assault to a charge of attempted murder.

During the winter months a crime of this serious nature would be more easily investigated. The event would be more shocking then as the population would be confined to residents. The scope of enquiries would be smaller as a result and the public response more forthcoming. In the summer, or holiday months, the scope was so much greater as two-thirds of those present in the area were 'visitors'.

The following day, Campbell was able to interview the victim. The woman was obviously bruised and swollen and her appearance was radically different from normal. She could only speak in a whisper and her eyes were almost closed, giving no expression to anything she said.

She identified herself as Mrs Karen Ratline, a widow and a school teacher. She was new to the area but had purchased a flat in readiness for the post she was about to take up at a local primary school. When she had been assured that her car had been brought to the safety of the police yard, Campbell asked her if she knew anyone in the area. Her answer was negative. She only knew the name of the lady who would be her school headmistress, Miss MacIvor.

What could she recall of her attacker, Campbell asked, what had he looked like?

The woman lay silent for a moment, a tear escaped from the corner of her eye.

"Tall, slim, dark oily hair, smelly." she said in succession as each feature occurred to her.

"Age?" the CID man asked.

"Young, thirties maybe."

"What was he wearing?"

"A dirty check jacket, like a thick shirt, a greenish blue colour. He had a knife."

"What did he do with this knife?" Campbell asked softly.

"He held it against my throat and I felt sure he wanted to kill me." the woman whimpered.

Campbell nodded. He had been told of the lacerations to her throat, chin and ears.

"Did he speak at all?"

"Not to me. He just swore a lot."

"Did you speak to him?" Campbell asked in the same soft tones.

"I pleaded with him to leave me alone but he never answered. He just hit me with his fist and then, when I tried to get up, he hit my head against a rock."

Campbell wondered what her assailant had done with his knife but did not expect his witness to know.

"Karen, were you aware of being sexually attacked by this man?"

This brought another tear and the woman closed the narrow gap of her eyes.

"Yes. I knew what he was doing and I screamed but he hit my head some more and I blacked out."

Campbell moved quickly to change the subject a little. He was aware that the doctor had arrived at the room door.

"We have your clothes, Karen. They will be examined at the police laboratory. I am told that you can expect to be in hospital for a week or two before you need outdoor clothing. I can speak to Miss MacIvor for you, if you wish. I know that she will help you. You are in safe hands, everyone here will be like a friend, believe me." Campbell assured her. "My job is to find this dangerous man. Do you remember anything unusual or particularly identifiable about him?"

"Stinking." she whispered.

"Yes, so you said."

"What kind of stink?" Detective Chief Inspector Adam roared down the phone line. "A fairground worker who stinks of oil and grease, a fisherman that stinks of fish, an alcoholic who stinks of drink or a gypsy who just stinks? Which is it?"

"I would go for the traveller, myself." Campbell answered soberly. "I am going to check out our local encampment right now."

"Good." Adam replied. "Did you find the rock or the knife?"

"No sir. We looked all over that place but the only thing with blood on it was the grass."

"Which you took?"

"Yes, of course, sir." Campbell lied. He would get some of the blood-stained grass before his boss made a visit.

Miss Jean MacIvor was shocked to hear of the attack on her latest member of staff. She wasted no time in attending at the hospital and introducing herself to Karen Ratline.

The two women talked for almost an hour with Jean MacIvor promising to stay in touch and to deal with all Karen Ratline's requirements. She had noted clothing sizes, preferred colours, likes and dislikes in fruit and sweets, favourite magazines and size in slippers. The only subject not discussed was the attack itself. The questions and conversation was obviously designed towards Karen Ratline's comfort and confidence. The injured woman felt that she had a friend in Jean MacIvor, as good a friend as she could have wished for. The head teacher had held her hand throughout and her sincere brown eyes had never left the face of the injured woman.

"You are so kind." Karen whispered. "You are on holiday. You should not be bothering with me so much."

"Nonsense." Jean MacIvor objected. "I never take a holiday from being who I am."

As Karen Ratline waved 'goodbye' to her departing visitor she wondered why Jean MacIvor had not asked about her relatives. She was not to know that Jean had asked the hospital staff that very question before the visit, only to be told that Karen had no relatives as far as they knew.

Douglas Campbell had collected the blood-stained grass from the scene of the crime and had visited the fixed encampment of travelling people, a camp situated well away from the scene of the crime. Now he spoke to the man at the Seamen's Mission regarding any fishermen who might fit the description of the assailant. There was no suggestion of a culprit from that exercise and Campbell was not looking forward to his boss's visit the following day. If there was a good side to this then it lay in the fact that Fleming was still on holiday up north with his family.

THREE

The Detective Chief Inspector took Campbell back to the hospital to re-interview Karen Ratline.

The thirty-seven years old victim was now more recognisable and more amenable to interview. Her improved condition helped the two CID men to ask their repertoire of questions but were disappointed to find that most of the answers they wanted were not available to the witness as she had quickly lost consciousness in the course of the assault and could not tell them anything about her assailant's actions after that point. What had he done with the knife, kept it or discarded it? What had he done with the rock? What direction had he taken when he had left? Had she seen another vehicle anywhere close? Of these things she knew nothing.

Was her attacker younger than her?

Yes, she thought he was five or ten years younger than her.

Had he distinguishing features, spots, scars, protruding teeth?

He had been unshaven, not a black beard, just unshaven. He had spoken, if only to curse, but had she heard any accent?

Not really an accent, just a clipped speech.

Had he actually been fishing when she stumbled across him?

She felt not. He had been crouched and holding a rod but their encounter had not surprised him in the way it had frightened her. Had he been waiting in readiness to attack her?

Perhaps.

"Had you ever seen this man before the attack?" Adam asked slowly, inviting Karen to give the matter some thought. She did.

"I had a good look at him, Chief Inspector, the sun was in his face and there was nothing familiar about him at all." she answered, retaining a puzzled frown.

"You're sure?" Adam pressed.

"Oh yes, I am sure I had never seen him before but why.." her voice tailed off.

"What's wrong, Miss?" Adam asked.

"He knew who I was. He referred to me as a 'Ratline bitch'. How did he know who I was?"

When Gordon Cargill failed to show up for work that Friday morning, Cathie Scott telephoned the Cargill house but no reply. Not only was it unlike Gordon not to come to the office, but he would normally inform Cathie of any reason he had for not doing so. Her employer had suffered a couple of heart attacks since Marjorie's death but his attendance at work had otherwise been constant.

She called the Police to enquire of any known reasons, such as road accidents. Accidents on the coast road would block the morning traffic for a while. The police officer said there had been none that morning but offered to have an officer check at Gordon's home.

Hamish MacLeod attended and soon found Cargill's Rover car still in the open garage. There was no response to the officer's knocking on the door. Hamish made his way around the large house, checking windows as he went. At the rear of the house he found the French doors to be wide open. There was nothing to suggest that these doors had been forced open and it appeared that they had been opened by the owner. The policeman entered the house calling out for Mr Cargill as he went but heard nothing. Inside the house nothing was obviously disturbed. The dinner dishes drying by the kitchen sink suggested that Cargill had dined alone. In the lounge there was no indication of anything being moved or switched on. The telephone handset was working. In the study there were papers spread across the desk as if they had been the subject of recent work. MacLeod read that Cargill was drawing up his role in the firm and there were hand-written paragraphs alongside the typing. These seemed to refer to Mr Cargill's will. A partly consumed whisky bottle stood on the desk beside an empty crystal glass. The impression given was of a work in progress, but where was the author?

Hamish MacLeod made his way up to the bedrooms

and found that all were neat and tidy. A suspense novel and spectacles lay beside a bedside lamp in a front room and gave the officer every reason to think that this was the owner's normal bedroom. The bed was neatly made, however, and had not been slept in. No other room produced Gordon Cargill and Hamish went back to the open French doors. From the doors a broken paving path led a twisting trail into the expanse of garden. The path ended by running around a garden pond. Here, face-down in the pond, was the clothed body of Gordon Cargill. On a garden bench nearby lay a twenty packet of cigarettes with a gold lighter on top of it.

When the doctor had been called the CID attended and found nothing to suggest foul play. The post-mortem would provide a medical answer to what had happened to the much respected solicitor.

The Fleming holiday was over and the time spent at Rhue, near Ullapool, had been a real pleasure as the sun had shone each day and relaxation had been as complete as they had hoped. Andrew Fleming scoured the local paper to learn of events he had missed while on holiday. He was saddened to see that Gordon Cargill had died of a heart attack. The popular old lawyer had always stopped to pass the time of day with Fleming anytime they had met. There had also been an attack on a young woman north of Corran Bay but few details were being given.

The following week Andrew Fleming would resume

work on nightshift and two weeks later, the children would both be attending primary school. Mary Fleming would also be attending school for she had procured a secretarial position at a local primary school, different but not distant, from the one her children would be attending. She was a little apprehensive but felt no real anxiety as Jean MacIvor, the head teacher, was someone already known to her.

Jean MacIvor had been busy on her new teacher's behalf and had purchased clothing, slippers and shoes for Karen Ratline. When Karen was being allowed home from hospital, Jean would call and collect her. Together they would go to the police station for Karen's car. The friendship being shown to Karen by a head teacher who scarcely knew anything about her, was restoring Karen Ratline's confidence and the will to pursue her career in this beautiful region. Would everyone else be this pleasant towards her?

The same thoughts had occurred to Jean MacIvor and she called Mary Fleming to see if she might join Jean and Karen for a meal in town once the patient was free to go home.

"Next week would not be a problem, Jean. Andy is due to be nightshift and I would need to be home for ten but that is better than the week after."

"Then we have a deal. I'll arrange a table at the usual place and you can help me to make Karen a bit more comfortable with Corran Bay. She has had a terrible time of it."

Jean explained to Mary the circumstances of the assault, as provided to her by Karen herself and described the extent of bruising and lacerations Karen had sustained.

"See what happens when that husband of yours goes on holiday." Jean joked.

"I must tell him what he has missed." Mary said mischievously. "She is such a pretty girl, your new teacher, I saw her picture in the local paper when they announced her appointment to the staff for the new term."

"A lot of people have said the same thing, Mary. She is a good person too. I think we will all get on well with her."

Andrew Fleming returned to work the following Monday evening. He had heard from Mary about the attack on a new teacher called Karen Ratline. Now he hoped to hear that Campbell and Adam had traced the man responsible.

"Are you kidding?" Hamish MacLeod said in sarcastic disbelief. "They have no idea who did it. They have been everywhere to look for this guy, the hospital, the youth hostel, the camping places, the travellers' camp, the Fishermen's Mission, the cheaper hotels and the ferry office. All they know about the man is that he is late twenties or early thirties, tall, slim, wears a blue or green check jacket and stinks."

"Where did it happen?" Fleming asked.

"On the road north, well out of town," Hamish answered. "Do you remember where that chap on the motor bike killed himself last year? He never took the bend and went into the trees, remember?"

"Yes." Fleming said with a nod of his head.

"About a mile farther north there is a series of short bends and a makeshift lay-by. The woman parked in that lay-by and went into the trees behind it to look out on the water. This guy was waiting in the bushes and jumped her."

Fleming looked at his colleague in disbelief.

"In the middle of nowhere there is a man in the bushes just waiting to pounce on her?"

"That's her story, a bhalaich."

"Was he soaking wet?" Fleming enquired.

Hamish laughed.

"Why?"

"Sounds like he had just arrived from Ireland." Fleming mused. "No wonder the CID are beat. Was there another car? How did the chap get there, miles from anywhere?"

Hamish shrugged.

"Maybe he was just waiting for anybody who stopped at that lay-by. It is the sort of place where folk would stop for the toilet." Hamish suggested.

Fleming looked at his colleague.

"Do the young ladies on Harris behave like that?"

"I don't know a bhalaich, I never waited in the bushes to find out."

Andrew Fleming knew of the lay-by but he had never stopped there. Hamish's suggestion of someone making a toilet stop would fit as a plausible reason to stop as the distance from there to the nearest toilet would be several miles in either direction. The following afternoon he drove north to the lay-by and parked there while he entered the rocky ground between the lay-by and the sea. To his left and right there were bushes of gorse, hawthorn, saplings and rhododendrons.

On his left he could see where the curtain of vegetation had been split apart to allow access. The school teacher might have begun the process but bulky CID men had increased and established the opening. Fleming walked through and quickly found a small clearing where the grass and small bushes had been flattened. The water's edge was not as close now and the undergrowth went around the clearing like a dense barrier. This was not a place to fish from.

He knew that Campbell and Adam were finished their examination of this spot and Fleming saw no reason for not doing some searching of his own. He studied the bark of the nearest trees and the criss-crossing branches which created the barrier around him. It appeared that the first person to enter the clearing by the route he had taken had not been the school teacher but her assailant.

This man had not used the same opening for his exit, however, he had simply crashed through from the clearing on a path of his own making. The bent bracken, the trailed hawthorn and the lay of the grass showed Fleming that, despite the considerable resistance, the assailant had simply broken through to the lay-by in his desperation to escape his crime. Fleming now devoted his attention to this new 'path' and beneath the jagged hawthorn he found something that he had not seen in years, a cycle clip.

He returned to the lay-by and stopped. 'Now what?' he wondered. 'Where did he go next?' The other side of the lay-by was at least as thick with vegetation but there was one narrow but definite opening. Fleming walked through, his eyes constantly searching the ground at his feet. There was far less undergrowth in this area, just trees and fairly short grass. The shortest grass and patches of bare mud formed a natural path through the trees. Andrew Fleming followed this, constantly searching for something to indicate recent human presence.

After 30 yards or so he noticed a pile of faeces about five feet to the right of the 'path'. It was weeks old but it could be human. Fleming remembered an account of how Reginald Spooner of Scotland Yard had worked for a time on a murder only to deduce from a pile of human faeces that the 'murder' had in fact been a suicide. Similar emotions might have led to this deposit.

Fleming continued and some seventy or eighty yards from the lay-by, Fleming found a patch of wet mud. It should have revealed footprints had anyone walked there recently. There were no footprints but there were cycle tyre impressions; the same cycle had passed in both directions. Again these were weeks old. Fleming returned to his car.

He drove north in the hope of seeing where the 'path' might emerge onto the public road but after three miles or so he could tell that the woodland path was more likely to be running parallel to the sea than the road. He continued, however, realising that the road would soon cross the regional boundary and leave his police jurisdiction.

A mile into the northern area he stopped at a local village shop and asked the elderly lady there, a Mrs MacTaggart, if she had heard of the attack on the woman at a lay-by six miles south. She told him that the whole village had been talking about it. It had been so shocking. Did they have the man yet?

Fleming informed her that he was a police officer from Corran Bay and he knew that they did not yet have the man. He asked her if she knew of any man living locally who went about on a bicycle? She replied that there were some. He then described a man in his early thirties, dark dirty hair and a checked shirt or jacket. That made the shopkeeper think.

"That sounds like the chap who was trying to steal my rolls about a month ago. He went away on a bike now that I think of it."

"Is that the only time you saw this man?" Fleming asked.

"Oh yes, he is not a customer and I do not know him,

so he can't be local." the old lady said with confidence. "How did he try to steal your rolls?"

The shopkeeper pressed a finger to her lips, as if considering where to begin.

"The bread rolls are delivered early in the morning, around six. If I am not quite here in time, or Ewan is early, he leaves them in the shed behind the shop. One morning, about a month ago, like I said, I arrived after Ewan had been here and I walked round to the shed. I suppose the man must have heard my footsteps, for he came out of the shed in a hurry, stared at me, then ran off round the far side of the building. I ran to the corner but by that time he was on his bike and tearing off down the road."

"Had he taken rolls with him?" Fleming asked.

"I think he did. I found two loose ones on the floor of the shed."

"Did you report that to the police?" Fleming asked, already feeling that she had not.

"No. I never did." she sighed. "I know that I should have but to be honest I felt a bit guilty. You see the order for rolls was occasionally a few short and I was beginning to suspect Ewan. Now I am inclined to believe that this stranger has been responsible. I have had no short orders since, you understand."

"Have you told Ewan about the roll thief?" Fleming asked.

"No, I haven't told anyone, except you." the old lady said as if she had surprised herself by realising this.

"I am thinking that Ewan may well have seen this man at some time. He would have no reason to suspect him of anything perhaps but he may well have seen him. Please ask him, will you?"

"Yes, I will. I won't be telling him about the rolls getting stolen, mind, but I will ask him if he has seen that man in the mornings."

"That would be kind of you. If Ewan has anything to say about this man, perhaps, you could let me know at Corran Bay Police Office."

Fleming was working nightshift that week, with no opportunity of speaking to Detective Sergeant Campbell, but he knew that little progress was being made in the case of rape and attempted murder of the school teacher.

Tomorrow was Thursday and Mary Fleming was due to keep a dinner appointment with her friend Jean and the new school teacher. Andrew Fleming was not unhappy with that arrangement. If his wife Mary and Karen Ratline were to become friends and work colleagues he felt confident of eventually tracing Karen's attacker.

The dining room of the hotel was pleasant. The tables and chairs were not in any way crowded and in the centre of the room a log fire burned beneath a copper canopy. Jean MacIvor had collected Karen Ratline from her flat to bring her to the hotel. They had met Mary Fleming at the car park.

The women found a corner table and were soon introducing themselves by way of home and work experience. Jean MacIvor was not married. Mary Fleming was married with two children at school and then it was Karen Ratline's turn to speak.

"You are not married, Karen?" Mary asked, suggesting an assumption.

"I was." Karen said reluctantly. "My husband died in a road accident three years ago."

Mary and Jean looked at each other in surprise. Jean had been told that her new member of staff was not married and had no children. She had told Mary this on the telephone.

"I am sorry, Karen." Jean said, stretching her hand across the table to place it on the back of Karen's hand. "Nobody has ever said as much to me. I was simply told that you had no husband."

Karen was staring at the table, her face blank of expression.

"I have no husband and I have no son." she said in a sad, wistful voice.

Jean and Mary again exchanged looks of surprise.

"Did you have a son, Karen?" Jean asked as sympathetically as she could.

"Oh yes. I had a baby boy called Callum. My husband never lived to see him." she said. "Callum was killed in an accident. A stone fell onto the pram when he was six months old."

Mary Fleming's face twisted in anguish.

"Is that what lies behind your move to Corran Bay?" Jean MacIvor asked, her hand still resting on Karen Ratline's.

"A fresh start, running from my nightmares. I suppose you are right, Jean."

"Only to find another nightmare waiting for you here." Jean said, shaking her head but continuing to look sympathetically at Karen. "You have been through the mill, Karen. Are you all right, emotionally, I mean?"

Only now did Karen look up from the table.

"I suppose time will tell. I am desperately needing to start work again, to have a room full of young faces with no bitterness towards me. My life needs purpose right now. I have lost all the intentions I had before. For whatever reason, I have been denied the right to find happiness with my husband and son. I either give in or I fight back and continue to put meaning and value into my living."

"You already sound like someone who could do that." Jean said reassuringly. "I am not sure that I could find that strength."

"As long as you both have enough strength to help me." Karen replied, smiling at the other two in turn.

A waiter took their order and brought them the drinks they wanted. This created a helpful hiatus in the conversation.

"Outside of the classroom, what do you enjoy doing?"

Mary asked, encouraging a move away from the morbid matters coming to light before the waiter had arrived.

"Oh well, I enjoy cooking and baking, Mary. I always have. I was the second youngest of four girls and my mother insisted that we all take a hand in the kitchen."

"Your dad wouldn't mind that?" Mary suggested, silently hoping that Karen's father had survived her upbringing.

"No. Dad was a miner. He could eat everything that was put in front of him." Karen remembered. "If I could not make a decent steak pie he would have disowned me."

"My father would have been the same." Mary said laughing.

"I envy you two girls with your cooking skills. It is something I never learned to do. My dad liked his food and my mother could cook well enough. I just never felt the need to learn from her." Jean said as if apologising for a failure.

"You were probably too busy." Karen commented, pleased to be giving some support. "Mary and I would be happy to show you, wouldn't we, Mary?"

"Yes, of course, once we get into the swing of our own jobs, we could get together on some project cooking. This hotel is great but we cannot expect to be coming here all the time." Mary said, purposefully implying a future togetherness.

"Where did you come from originally, Karen?" Jean asked.

"I was born in Lanark, at the William Smellie Hospital actually, but my parents stayed near Stonehouse when I was young. I think they imagined us all going to Glasgow University or Jordanhill College but only two of us did."

"Did you teach in Glasgow?" Mary asked.

"Yes, to begin with. I worked at three different primary schools before I met Fraser."

"Your husband?" Jean enquired.

"Yes. Fraser was an insurance guy, always coming into the school to check on the latest theft of the computer. Only the head teacher had a computer in these days but there were plans to create an education network for the whole of the city. Every school was going to have them and be linked up. Lots of talk but no money, sort of idea. Then they remembered about regionalisation in 1975 and the idea was shelved temporarily. By that time Fraser and I were 'an item' as they say in the movies. We got married in 1977 and bought a house in East Kilbride."

"I thought you were further east than that." Jean objected. "I don't remember the address or the school, but you were back in the countryside, I thought."

"I only did that when the baby was due, Jean. I wanted to deliver little Callum in Lanark, so I went to stay near the village of Forth. An aunt and uncle of mine had a small holding there. I was still there when Fraser was killed. I was there when Callum was born; I was back home with my folks when Callum died and I was still there when I applied for your vacancy at Corran Bay."

"And the East Kilbride house?" Jean asked. "Is it still your home address?"

"No. It stopped being my home after I lost Fraser and Callum. When my application for the vacancy here was accepted, I sold that house. I just wanted away from that area for a while. I even wanted away from my folks' house near Stonehouse. The flat I have bought in Corran Bay is my own. The house sale and Fraser's life insurance helped that side of things, just about the only good to have come out of my recent life."

"Think of it as a basis for better things to come." Jean suggested.

FOUR

Andrew Fleming would not normally pay much attention to his wife's reports of her social activities but her account of meeting Karen Ratline received his full attention. He wanted to know as much as he could about this lady victim but he was careful not to question Mary beyond the information being told to him.

The following week he began to work on late-shift and he soon found Detective Sergeant Douglas Campbell.

"Have you caught up with the guy who attacked the school teacher yet, Dougie?"

"No Andy. I still think we are looking for one of these travellers but of course, the one we need will have scampered." Campbell replied with a tone of hopelessness.

"What if he belongs north of here? Had you considered that?" Fleming suggested.

"Yeah. We have a general request for any traveller camps around this area to be searched. So time will tell."

"What if this guy had a bike?" Fleming asked. "He doesn't seem to have had a vehicle."

"Suppose he could have had a motor bike." Campbell conceded.

"No. I meant a push bike, Dougie, an ordinary two wheeler."

"What gives you that idea?" Campbell said with a smirk, as if the thought was ridiculous.

"Maybe just the fresh tyre tracks about 40 yards north of the crime scene." Fleming said evenly.

"North?" Campbell said in surprise. It had not occurred to him that someone would make an escape northwards. For miles there was nowhere to go.

"Yes, north." Fleming confirmed. "In fact he made a toilet stop before he left."

Campbell looked at Fleming with a mixture of admiration and disgust.

"I might have known you would visit the crime scene. You must be part Apache." he said before leaving, presumably to call his boss, Raymond Adam.

Fleming headed out on foot and walked to the local travellers' encampment where he had an old friend. Big Jock McGregor was now 72 years of age and widowed. The man had been a worker all his days and Andy had liked the old man since learning that they had once worked in the same forest in the Carron valley. It was only recently that Jock had confided in Andy that he had been diagnosed with stomach cancer. The well-respected elder of the camp had no wish to be considered less able and had not told the others around him.

"Hello John," Fleming called as he approached the big

man sitting outside his caravan. "I brought your favourite biscuits. Are you still able to eat them?"

"Of course." the big man replied, laughing. "How are things with you? How did the holiday go?"

When John had heard of the Fleming holiday and Fleming had heard of John's radiotherapy treatment, both men went into John's caravan for as John said, "These biscuits are best wi' a cup o' tea."

Fleming sat on the near side of the table for he knew that Jock McGregor liked to sit at the side facing the caravan door.

"You have had the CID round a couple of times, I believe." Fleming said as the big man poured the tea into fine bone china cups.

"Aye, your colleague Campbell was here asking around the camp for all blokes between twenty and forty. He never quite described the man he was after but said he was likely in his early thirties."

Jock put the cups down on the table and opened the packet of biscuits, spilling some onto a plate.

"I asked him why he had come here to enquire after this man for we all knew where the woman had been attacked. It was in the paper. He said the woman had described the man as 'stinking'." He glanced at Fleming to see the look of disapproval. "He was pretty much accusing us of being suspects because the guy was stinking. How is that for damn cheek, Andy?"

"That's Campbell, right enough. About as subtle as a

firing squad and quite wrong, Jock. If Campbell was right I wouldn't be sitting here and I wouldn't visit old Maggie McPhee yonder either. As you say, Jock, the man has a damn cheek." Fleming took a sip of his tea. "What about the attack on the young woman, Jock, have you any thoughts on what might have happened there?"

"That is not the sort of thing that young travelling folks would do, Andy. It has happened before, mind you, but on very few occasions and usually between families. Attacking a stranger for no good reason is just not our way. There is usually some sort of logic to anything one of our boys do. My own two sons are big enough to take on anybody but they have never harmed anybody yet."

"You still haven't told them about your stomach cancer, have you Jock?" Fleming said quietly.

Jock shook his head.

"There will come a time for that." he said soberly. Fleming had often considered that old MacIain, chieftain of the Macdonalds of Glencoe, might have looked and sounded a lot like Jock McGregor, before that old man was treacherously murdered in his bed in 1692.

"No Andy," Jock continued. "I think your man is a loner and maybe a bit loose in the head."

"The man concerned dresses in a green or blue checked shirt or jacket, maybe that quilted type." Fleming suggested.

"Well, we have both worn one of them at some time." Jock remarked.

Andrew Fleming laughed.

"You think this guy is a lumberjack?"

"No, I don't think he is wise enough to be a woodman." Jock answered, smiling. "But how did he come by the jacket? Stole it more likely."

Fleming nodded.

"Do you remember a woman that used to visit Corran Bay years ago? She would try to tell fortunes for money? She might have had a bairn with her."

"You mean the Galloway seer?" Jock said with surprise.

"So you did know her?" Fleming replied.

"I knew her man even better. I worked with Mike Galloway on the Cruachan Dam twenty years ago and before that on the wood down by Glendaruel. His wife would be the woman you mean."

"Could she tell fortunes?" Fleming asked.

"She told Mike that the Manchester United players would not get back from Germany. That was before the Munich disaster in 1958. She had aye said that the Russians would put a man into space and that the Americans would land on the moon. She seemed to have the gift right enough but she never saw Mike's death coming. Yes, he died a quick one. Lightning hit when he was trying to release a wire hawser. That woman went clean out of her mind." Jock said dreamily, his thumb running round the edge of his tea cup. "That would be about '63".

"And the boy?" Fleming asked.

"No idea. She just took off with that boy and I have never heard of her since."

Fleming wondered.

"Was she the type of woman to know about the covenanters?" he asked.

Jock turned and looked at Fleming.

"God help us, Andy. You have the gift as well." Jock said without laughing.

"How so?"

"She had always claimed to have covenanter ancestry. When Mike got killed by lightning she said that an ancestor of hers that fought with Munro in Ireland had been killed by lightning. He lifted up his sword at the wrong time, it seems. Her family had been heavily into the covenanting scene, according to her. Mike aye said she was still carrying the bitterness of it all." Jock remembered.

"So she was already a bit weird?" Fleming suggested.

"Yeah, she was weird. Even Mike thought so. He used to tell me that she had that boy of theirs sleeping with her when Mike was away. Mike was away a lot of course but the boy was about twelve years of age and simple. He never went to any school at all." Jock said but then corrected himself. "Well I think he tried the school at first, but the kids just laughed at him and he never went back. His mother took him away. They moved about a lot and they never stayed beside other folk."

"But you haven't seen either of them for twenty years?" Fleming asked.

"That's right. Have you met them?" Jock asked.

"Not the boy," Fleming answered. "But maybe I have seen the mother."

Fleming proceeded to relate to Jock the tale of the woman he had witnessed when he had gone ashore from his boat. He also mentioned the punctured inflatable dinghy.

"So she wasn't alone." old Jock commented.

"Does that sound like your Galloway seer?" Andrew Fleming asked.

"Everything her husband had to say about her made her sound crazy." Jock said thoughtfully. "And she mentioned a covenanter's stane when you heard her. Mike's wife had this thing about covenanters, so it does sound like her."

"What was her name, do you remember?" asked Fleming.

"Jessie, Jessie Sorbie. I cannae mind the boy's name." Jock said with candour.

"Where would that woman be staying?" Fleming asked, expecting no suggestions.

"Maybe in a caravan or even a cave, Andy. She hated the thought of living in a house, apparently. The covenanters used caves a lot, some caves are still there, in Lanarkshire, Ayrshire and Wigtonshire. There is one that was used by William Wallace and then later by the covenanters, but there are no covenanters' caves about here. There could well be some caves just the same. This area has seen its own share of outlaws from the law down through the years."

"A McGregor would know about things like that." Fleming said mischievously. Without replying or looking at Jock.

Jock just smiled.

"We didn't all have castles to run home to."

South of Corran Bay lay a makeshift campsite restricted to small tents. The square of grass could not really be referred to as a field but it had once been part of a farm field. Now an old retired couple made a seasonal income from the only piece of land they owned. The only source of water in the camp was a single tap fixed to the wall of an old outhouse and beneath it lay a Belfast sink. There were no toilets and the site was not used by families. The regular users were hikers, students and any young people with little money to spend.

During the current spell of hot weather the tiny campsite was crammed to full capacity.

James Beattie and Tom Jackson were two Glasgow art students who shared a small tent fairly close to the solitary water tap. Realising the crowd that might develop in the morning the pair rose early and went to the tap to wash while others still slept. They would also fill their camping kettle.

Their idea was successful and for several minutes they seemed to have the place to themselves. As James Beattie turned away from the tap he found two pretty teenage girls standing a short distance from him, one wearing a light robe but the other wearing only jogging pants. He stared open-mouthed at the girl's bare breasts and felt awkward and embarrassed. The girls merely smiled and said 'Bonjour'. Jackson wasted no time in giving them exclusive use of the tap.

Through the split in the tent door flap the boys watched the girls washing and brushing teeth before returning to their tent. The experience was the sole topic of conversation once the kettle boiled.

In the evening of that day the Glasgow students were drinking beer in a Corran Bay lounge when they realised that the two French girls were also in the lounge. As they drank more and returned to the earlier topic of conversation the students encouraged each other to use their schoolboy French on the girls and walk them back to the campsite.

As it happened, both girls had a better than average understanding of English and spoke the language well. Conversation was easy. They introduced themselves as Suzanne and Denise, Denise being the one with no bath robe. They all left the lounge together when the premises closed in the early hours and walked together through the town. As they began to walk down the unlit coast road Tom Jackson walked in front with Suzanne while James Beattie and Denise were together behind them.

These pairings had resulted from the conversation in the lounge where Suzanne and Tom had recognised themselves as more serious and responsible while James and Denise were obviously more free-spirited. As Tom and Suzanne carried on a sensible conversation and made progress, the pair behind were inclined to find things to laugh at and lagged behind.

Darkness had fallen but at this time of year that did not mean total black-out and it was possible to see the immediate vicinity at all times. Soon Tom and Suzanne had distanced themselves enough from James Beattie and Denise that the couples could no longer see each other. It was now that Beattie became bolder and more intimate. He held Denise in a restraining hug and kissed her forcefully. She offered no resistance but suspected that her companion was impatient and not motivated by romance. Those suspicions were confirmed when Beattie pushed his hand upwards inside her sweatshirt top, coarsely fondling her breasts. She began to protest but Beattie brought his left hand around her head to cover her mouth. Denise wriggled to free herself from the man's grip but he became more physical, pushing her from the roadway and down onto the grass verge at the roadside.

Beattie began to remove her loose fitting sports trousers. Despite her kicking wildly with her legs, he was succeeding. She bit the hand that momentarily slipped off her mouth and Beattie swore at her. He punched her on her forehead. For a few moments she was dazed but soon realised that Beattie had removed her pants and trousers. His left hand was again firmly over her mouth.

She fought and struggled as well as she could but Beattie was now incensed and committed to raping the girl. He paid no heed to her struggling and weeping. Again, when the weeping became annoying to him, he struck her with his fist. Her body relaxed but she remained conscious.

Beattie heard the sound of an approaching vehicle and quickly got to his feet, fastening his trousers. He set off running down the coast road, away from the girl and the car that came round the corner behind him in time to catch him in its headlights. The lights also caught the prostrate naked figure of Denise as she lay still on the grass.

The driver of the car stopped beside her. He was a local fisherman with a boat berthed down the coast, beyond the campsite. The man realised that what he had come across was not some courting couple. He cautiously approached the girl on the ground and asked her if she was okay.

"Non, non. He rape me." she complained. Her weeping began again.

"Bloody thought so." the fisherman remarked. "C'mon lass. Get yer clothes on. I'll take ye tae the police."

Douglas Campbell had no objection to being paid overtime but he felt quite bitter when he was forced to leave his warm bed and earn it. The phone call from the office brought him down to attend to a reported case of rape on a French girl on holiday. On his way to the police office he had already considered the number of nomadic persons in the area, the possibility that the French girl had no English and the unsociable demeanour of a duty doctor summoned from his bed for an examination of the girl.

Matters improved greatly for Campbell when he discovered that a genuine witness existed in the form of a local honest fisherman; Denise spoke perfect English, or at least as good as his; and the duty doctor was the ever enthusiastic Doctor Merchiston. A female police officer had also been summoned for corroboration of the victim's statement and the doctor's examination. Samples were collected for forensic examination.

Campbell felt elated when he heard the description of the suspect as given by Denise and the fisherman. The man responsible was tall and thin. A lot of men are tall and thin but Campbell had a habit of joining unrelated dots. He could see how this could be the man for the rape of Karen Ratline.

Attending at the campsite with uniformed officers, Campbell found James Beattie and Tom Jackson in the process of dismantling their tent in readiness to leave. A distressed Suzanne was pleading with a sympathetic Jackson to help her find her friend, Denise. Beattie was apprehended and the other two were taken to the police office for interview.

James Beattie chose to say nothing but the case against him built satisfactorily when Suzanne and Jackson spoke the truth. Detective Sergeant Campbell asked Jackson where his mate Beattie had been on an earlier date, the date of Karen Ratline's attack, but Tom Jackson had no idea.

Beattie appeared at court later that morning and was remanded in custody. Campbell had been so bold as to suggest that the accused may be able to assist with other outstanding cases. He had also said as much to Detective Chief Inspector Raymond Adam when he called him at 9 a.m. to boast of his night's work.

The Chief Inspector had grunted in enthusiasm.

FIVE

Fleming considered the weekly rest days falling between lateshift and dayshift to be useless now that both the children and Mary were attending school during the day. He was on his own and set out with the six creels that a friend had given him. He had salted herring to bait the creels and he knew a rocky area where he could afford to leave the creels for up to a week in the hope of catching some lobsters.

As he set off up Loch Linne he breathed in the good warm air and thought of how the temperature seemed to rise with each passing day. Today there was no wind at all and by the time he returned he could expect to have tanned considerably.

Baiting his creels and laying them in line from a heavy piece of pig iron, acting as an anchor, he marked the position of the last creel with a marker buoy. Then he took The Marlin out to deeper water and let her drift while he cast out a weighted line of lures in the hope of catching mackerel. The mackerel were there and he brought them out in sixes and sevens at a time. So engrossed was he in his success that he failed to notice just how much The

Marlin had drifted towards the shore. It was now in line with the headland where he had previously gone ashore.

On noticing his position he recalled the crazy old woman who may, or may not, have been the Galloway seer. Fleming purposefully allowed the boat to drift even closer before dropping anchor and taking down his inflatable from the cabin roof. He quietly rowed to shore and tied the dinghy to some exposed roots. Without looking around him at all he went into the undergrowth at the same point as before but this time he waited and watched his dinghy. After five minutes nobody had come near to the dinghy and he continued through the bushes and trees beyond the spot where the old woman had previously wailed over a wood fire.

The intense humidity was bringing midges by the thousand to attack his exposed arms and face as he brushed through the bushes and bracken. The air felt heavy and calm and these conditions made two things highly likely, midges and thunder.

Somewhere up ahead of him Fleming could hear a male voice calling out the same word repeatedly. It sounded like 'Mummy', but it was certainly not distinct. The voice was that of an adult but child-like in its plaintiveness.

Suddenly the forest was lit up by a moment of intense light and Fleming had already turned around when the heavy peel of thunder came. Somewhere behind him a woman screamed in terror. He guessed that he had just heard the 'Galloway seer' once again.

The occasional heavy raindrop fell on him as he reached his dinghy and began to row purposefully for The Marlin. He got the dinghy onto the cabin roof and was beginning to attach his rear canopy when the downpour started in earnest. Fleming stood in the cabin, watching the rain bouncing on the non-slip decks outside, grateful to have missed the worst of the rain but frustrated that he had not seen the source of the calling and screaming. Another flash of lightning lit up the area and he thought the scream was repeated somewhere in the depth of the wood. The rain persisted for another thirty minutes before Fleming was prepared to venture out and pull up his anchor.

Once home again, Fleming heard from Mary that Detective Sergeant Campbell had been at the primary school to arrange for Karen Ratline to attend an identity parade the following day. A suspect had been found in the form of a young man answering the description of her attacker.

"Good news, eh Andy?" Mary suggested.

"I think not," he answered as he shook his head. "I think his suspect is the man who attacked a young French girl the other night. He is tall and thin with dark hair but not similar in other respects. A thousand young men in this area are tall and thin with dark hair."

"But they are not all rapists." Mary objected.

"No. You're quite right. There may only be two."

Fleming said with a confidence that Mary chose not to dispute.

"How is Karen Ratline taking to her new life here in Corran Bay, or is it too early to tell?" Fleming asked.

"She could have done without this invitation to an identity parade," Mary said with some disgust. "But she is enjoying the school and is well liked by the other teachers. She seems to be a natural with children too, according to Jean. Nobody has ever raised the subject of her rape, of course, nobody until today, that is."

Fleming looked at his wife for a few moments as she continued to prepare vegetables for the dinner.

"You should ask her out here some evening, Mary. I would hate to become a figure of mistrust by association."

"You mean you could speak to her without talking about her attack?" Mary said with heavy scepticism.

"I could. I would actually want to avoid the subject unless she chose to raise it herself. I just have a feeling that knowing Karen a bit better would help me in this particular case." he said, trying to sound reassuring.

"It's not your case, Andy, remember? As for inviting Karen to our house, we'll see. Maybe if she doesn't react too badly to this identity thing, then I could find an opportunity that suits an invitation." Mary said. "Apparently she cooks a good curry. I have already suggested that she teaches me how. You like curry, don't you?"

Fleming was nodding pensively, at what exactly, Mary was not sure.

Ewan MacLeod, the bread delivery man, did not mind hanging about on a fine morning to wait for Mrs MacTaggart, but on a wet morning he would prefer to be on his way. It was only 5.50 a.m. and he knew that he was early but he marched round the small village shop with a tray of rolls and some wrapped loaves. He laid these out in the outhouse behind the shop and was returning to his open van when he saw the dark haired figure in a green and blue checked heavy shirt cycling away from the van. Ewan ran down to the open rear doors and immediately knew that the man had just stolen one of his loaves. The loaves filled each tray in a uniform formation and there was a tell-tale empty space at the corner of a board that he knew had been full.

The man on the cycle turned off the road some distance away and rode directly into the forest, something that did not look possible. Ewan was aware of the story Mrs MacTaggart had told him of her rolls being taken by a similar looking man. She had also lost a few newspapers the same way apparently.

He closed the van doors and would have driven away but for a call from further along the road. Ewan turned to find Mrs MacTaggart running down to meet him.

"I saw him, Ewan. That man on the bike, I saw him."

"Don't worry Mrs MacTaggart, it is only a loaf of bread. Just one loaf."

"No, Ewan there is more to that fellow than a loaf of bread. I will phone the policeman that was after him. I still have his number."

Douglas Campbell had rounded up six volunteer stand-ins for his identity parade. They all could be described as tall, slim young men with dark hair. James Beattie was invited to join them in a numbered line, adopting any position he chose to occupy in that line. He imagined that the man at No. 4 looked most like him so he asked to be placed beside him at No. 3. When this had been done, Karen Ratline was brought to the officer conducting the identity parade and introduced to him and others present as the victim of an assault one month earlier.

The sergeant conducting the parade was not someone who had previously worked on any aspect of the rape case involving Karen Ratline. He stood alongside Karen and explained what was required of her. She should look carefully at each man in turn and allow consideration to the fact her assailant's personal appearance and clothing may have been changed in the interim. If she wished to see any man from one side or the other, if she wished to hear the person speak, then she should address these requests to the sergeant.

Karen Ratline walked slowly down the line of men, looking carefully into the face of each one without actually stopping at any time. When she completed the 'inspection' she turned to the sergeant and told him in clear, distinct tones, "The man who attacked me is not there."

"Are you sure, Mrs Ratline?" the sergeant asked.

"Quite certain. If my attacker was there I would know him, but he is not one of these men." Karen Ratline said firmly.

When Andrew Fleming began work on Friday morning he found that Mrs MacTaggart had called for him the previous day. He immediately called the elderly lady, knowing that she would be in her shop. She told him of the theft of a loaf from the baker's van by the very man who had stolen her rolls and fitted the description of the man he was looking for.

"He was on his bike again and still wearing that same dirty blue and green thing that he had on before." the old lady explained with disgust.

"Has Ewan reported this theft to your local police, Mrs MacTaggart?"

"No, Mr Fleming, he says it isn't worth the bother for one loaf, but I know there is more to this man than stealing bread." she said, trying in her own subtle way, to draw more information from Fleming.

"One day we will all know what there is to this man, Mrs MacTaggart. In the meantime try to think of any customers or others around the village who could be related to this chap." Fleming asked, trying in his own subtle way, to restore the esteem of the lady in the village shop.

It was later that forenoon that Fleming was summoned to the room of Chief Inspector Stewart Mackellar. Already in the room with Mackellar, were Detective Chief Inspector Adam and Detective Sergeant Campbell.

"Well, Fleming, it seems you are up to your freelancing again," Mackellar began. "You seem to be investigating thefts in another police area. What's this about a Mrs MacTaggart calling here for you because someone stole a loaf of bread from her delivery van?"

"What gives you the idea that I am investigating the theft of her bread, sir?" Fleming asked, as if the suggestion was ridiculous.

"Why did you ask her to phone you if it happened again? That's what the woman apparently gave as her reason for calling it in here." Mackellar said stiffly.

"Yes, I did. The person who is stealing her rolls or bread is a man who answers the description of Karen Ratline's assailant."

"That's a CID case, Fleming. It has nothing to do with you." Campbell complained, obviously smarting from his failed identification parade.

"So why had the CID not spoken to Mrs MacTaggart?" Fleming asked with a serious look on his face. "Her shop is five miles north of your crime scene but it is still closer than any other shop."

"It is in a different police area, Fleming." Mackellar blurted.

"When I find this stinking man in the blue/green jacket, I will tell him that." Fleming said with annoyance.

Detective Chief Inspector Adam was silent during the discourse but now he spoke and did so calmly.

"Do you have anything to tell us at this stage, Andrew?"

Fleming took a deep breath and looked at Adam.

"No sir. If I had enough to be worth mentioning, I would have done so, but I have no name for this man and I have not seen him myself. At the moment I am finding coincidences but it is all fur and feathers with no real evidential value."

"When did you become an expert on the value of evidence?" Mackellar asked.

Fleming looked at his Chief Inspector with a cold stare.

"I've aye been an expert on the value of evidence. There's mair tae being a detective than wearing a disposable suit." he said in a barely concealed rage.

Raymond Adam chuckled to himself. He had heard this from Fleming before and had never been an admirer of the deskbound Mackellar.

"I will leave it to yourself to inform us of any substantiated evidence you might have." Adam said firmly. He was speaking as much to Mackellar and Campbell as he was to Fleming.

"You can count on it, sir." Fleming answered before storming out.

Adam turned to Mackellar and Campbell.

"We can expect to hear from Mr Fleming when he has more than 'fur and feathers', gentlemen. I'll settle for that."

Fleming kept a low profile for the rest of that shift, allowing himself to cool off from his verbal joust with

Mackellar. Insubordination was a discipline offence and he had always sailed close the wind where senior officers, as opposed to superior officers, were concerned. He was finished work before Mary would be finished at the school so he went home and changed clothes before driving north to see Mrs MacTaggart. He had no way of knowing how long he might need the lady to stay faithful to his cause.

He parked outside the small shop and went in to see his witness.

"Just where did he ride into the trees, Mrs MacTaggart?" Fleming asked when he had coaxed the shopkeeper to come out to her front door.

"Do you see yon tree with the branch hanging down to the ground?" she asked, pointing northwards along the road. "Well, it was just this side of that tree."

"I'll go and have a look for myself." Fleming said. "I'll be back to let you know what I find."

He walked up the road and cut into the trees where Mrs MacTaggart had indicated. To his surprise he found that a narrow path led through the densely populated forest. He followed the path, reassured by the occasional mark of a bicycle tyre. On two occasions he had to cross forestry roads to maintain the route he was following. The trail led uphill and down but the cyclist had followed this path for there were his cycle marks crossing a small burn.

It did not occur to Fleming that he had spent an hour on this trail and still had not caught up with the bread thief. Perhaps he was getting closer to his destination for he detected a smell of burning wood in the air. Finally he saw a rising plume of smoke up ahead.

The path curled to his left and descended around a raised bluff of ground that was straight ahead of Fleming and in line with the smoke. He elected to move forward off the path and looked down onto a small clearing where a circle of stones contained a log fire. Balanced precariously over the fire was a filthy looking cooking pan. An old black bicycle was propped against a tree beyond the fire but there was nobody to be seen. Fleming was aware of noises beneath him and pulled closer to the edge of the overhang. The drop of fifteen feet or so contained an opening in the rock face. Here was the cave Fleming had hoped to find. He drew back from the edge and it was just as well for a man, tall and slim with dark hair and several days' growth of beard, emerged from the cave to add a handful of logs to the fire after removing the heated pan. The man was stripped to the waist and never noticed Fleming as he returned to the cave with the cooking pan. The woman was in the cave, Fleming thought, for he could hear her making sounds of singing or simple pleasure. Then he heard the young man speaking quietly to her. This was followed by a raised voice, sounding identical to what Fleming had heard on the night of the thunder. In tones of childish pleasure the young man was calling out, "Bunny, Bunny, Bunny". Fleming drew slowly back and began to retrace his steps.

The voice had been that of an adult but the nature of the shouting had been like a child with a toy or an ice cream. It would be reasonable to assume that this pair ate rabbit on a regular basis but surely the novelty had long gone? In these bleak surroundings there could be few alternatives to rabbit on the menu.

Fleming reported what he had found to Mrs MacTaggart before setting off home. Mary was less than amused when he arrived late for his dinner. He was treated to a lukewarm meal and a very cold shoulder.

Karen Ratline sat nervously in the waiting room of the doctor's surgery. She had been there two weeks earlier to give blood and other samples. When her name was called she could not walk quickly enough for her own satisfaction. She must know the truth.

Doctor Susan Wallace looked at her and smiled. She realised just how tense her patient had been while awaiting these results. Taking a gentle hold of her by both hands, the doctor told her, "You have nothing to fear. You are not pregnant. You seem to be clear of any significant infection. Have you finished the antibiotics?"

"Yes. I have taken them all." Karen said as her smile appeared and her eyes moistened.

"You must have been very uptight for the past fortnight. I don't suppose you have spoken to anyone about your concerns, apart from myself, I mean?"

"No. I do not find it easy to talk to other people about that night, not yet anyway."

"How are you managing at the school?" the doctor asked.

"I am actually enjoying it and it is teaching me that other people have their own worries for themselves and their children. I know some parents with whom I can empathise in a real sense. Before my own disasters began I had no idea just how raw emotional wounds could be." Karen said, squeezing the fingers that still held her own. "I hope I can be as understanding of others as you have been of me."

"I am sure you can," Susan Wallace said confidently. "Now let me check these fingernail indentations behind your ear, again. Have you told anyone about these?"

"No. I have only told you, doctor. I never told the police either. They had interviewed me before I realised these cuts were there."

Susan Wallace looked at the back of both ears and reported that they were 'healing nicely'.

"I think you can afford to turn your attention to your pupils, Karen. You seem to have a clean bill of health, other than any flashback memories of course. If these become a problem for you, do not simply ignore them. I have answers for that sort of thing too."

On Saturday morning Fleming discovered that Douglas Campbell was on duty with enquiries to conduct as a result of some prodding by Detective Chief Inspector Raymond Adam. There seemed to be no way of avoiding Dougie Campbell.

"Have you found your bread thief yet?" Campbell asked in a conciliatory sort of tone.

"Yes. I know where he stays but the shopkeeper and the delivery driver have no wish to pursue theft charges against the chap and haven't reported these thefts to their local police." Fleming responded.

"So where does this guy stay?" Campbell asked.

"He stays with his mother in a cave deep in the woods." Fleming said flatly.

Campbell stared at him.

"This some kind of fairy story? You won't tell me the truth, just Raymond Adam, is that your game?" Campbell asked with heat in his voice.

Fleming remained calm.

"If I told Raymond Adam that someone desperate enough to lie in wait for a bread delivery at five-fifty in the morning was someone who stayed in a cave deep in the woods, would his immediate response be to think I was telling him a fairy tale?" Fleming said. "I have told you where a bread thief lives. He was not wearing his blue and green jacket when I saw him but he had it when stealing the bread. I know where he lives and if you want to see for yourself then I can take you. Just remember that he is not wanted for anything solid. He simply fits the description of Karen Ratline's attacker."

Campbell realised that Fleming was serious about the man in the cave.

"Okay. I could drive you up there." Campbell suggested.

"You could drive us up there, Dougie, but we would be walking for over an hour to reach his cave. Are you up for that?" Fleming asked mischievously. He knew that Campbell did no more walking than he needed to.

"Haven't got time for that." Campbell said. "Is there not another way to get there?"

"I can get there by boat," Fleming offered. "It is well up the loch but the walking bit would be shorter."

"When can you go?" Campbell asked.

"Monday afternoon. I will be checking my creels on Monday afternoon. They are in the same area."

"And you would take me with you?" Campbell asked hesitantly, knowing that Fleming would be off-duty at the time he had in mind.

"Sure." said Fleming. "Remember your camera, a torch, sample bags and the like. I don't think you will want to be going there too often."

"Thanks Andy." Campbell said enthusiastically. This venture with Fleming would please Adam, no doubt about that.

"I know I said I would invite her, Andy, but the woman has been quite withdrawn on anything outside of the school curriculum. She obviously has had a lot on her mind. I will ask her to visit once I see her looking and sounding more relaxed. Jean MacIvor feels the same about Karen, the girl is not ready for socialising yet." Mary Fleming said, sounding quite emphatic. "Her attacker is still out there, remember? How would anybody feel in these circumstances?"

"Yeah, okay, Mary, I will just have to be patient." Fleming agreed.

"That'll be a first." she mumbled to herself. "Anyway she is going down to her parents for the weekend. She wants to visit the graves of her husband and baby."

Karen Ratline had indeed decided to go 'home' for the weekend and shortly after finishing her school day she was putting her suitcase into her car.

As she drove out of town and headed south she realised how much it would mean to be seeing her parents again. There was always something safe and comforting about being with one's parents. She switched on her cassette player and listened to some Abba songs, their music usually raised her spirits.

The evening was clear and sunny and it was hardly surprising that people should be walking beside the road, miles from town, but there was one pair that made her look in her rear view mirror after passing them. The woman was older with long untended grey hair and her clothes did not look new or clean, but it was her companion who had caused the distraction. He was young enough to be her son and he was tall and slim with black hair. There was no green and blue check jacket, just a T shirt and floppy black trousers. He still looked familiar and Karen shivered involuntarily, despite the warmth in her car. She certainly did not stop to satisfy her curiosity.

No people on Earth knew better than Karen's parents just how much she had suffered from the deaths of her husband in a road accident and then her baby boy in that terrible accident at the cemetery. Both her parents were good people, old Lanarkshire stock for the past four hundred years. Generations for whom the business of living with trial and turbulence had been expected and quite normal. They had bolstered the flagging spirit of their daughter Karen through the past year, taking her from near-suicide to some prospect of returning to a worthwhile career and some personal happiness.

They listened with interest as she described the highland setting of the primary school and the friendly folks she worked with. The children all seemed happy and innocent. Most were imaginative and intelligent. She was sure that teaching such children would prove rewarding.

Karen would have chosen to keep the attack on her a secret from her parents but the incident had made the national press and was no secret to them or their neighbours. They asked how she was coping with the effects of that incident.

She made light of it as best she could and told them that she had been foolish to stop at such an isolated spot on her own. She would not be doing that again. Her new friends had rallied round, she told her parents. Starting school again had pushed the matter further back in her consciousness.

"Tomorrow we will go to Hamilton, Karen, and I hope we can find some beautiful flowers for the cemetery. We might even find something new in the way of clothes. What do you think?" her mother suggested as if the pleasure ought to be mutual.

On Sunday morning she accompanied her parents to church and met several local villagers who were keen to speak to her and hear how she liked working again. All seemed to have nothing but good wishes for her future and told her so.

After lunch she returned with her parents to the local cemetery where a new section had been opened five years earlier. The newer headstones, her husband's among them, glinted in the sunshine. There was a separate area for child graves but Karen had wanted Callum to be buried with his dad. He had been visiting his daddy's grave when he died, after all.

After tidying up some blown leaves Karen filled the brass topped bowl with water and inserted the flowers she had bought until there was no space left to be filled. Her parents watched her carefully as she did this and when she stepped back to admire her work she looked serious but not sad.

"They will always be with me." she said softly. "I see a growing Callum in every little boy at school."

She turned to her parents and put an arm behind each of them.

"Let's go and leave them in peace." she suggested without any display of grief. Her father nodded his head. Perhaps his daughter was a Thomson after all. She had not even glanced at the memorial stone, now repaired, that had brought about her baby son's early death.

After Sunday lunch together as a family, Karen left her parents and drove north to ensure her readiness for work on Monday morning.

When Monday morning came Michael Mowatt was walking behind a motor mower set to keep the grass in the cemetery at a height of one centimetre. Done regularly this prevented the daisies from breaking the uniform carpet of green grass. He took a pride in his work and when Michael turned the corner into the 'new' section, his heart sank.

A bouquet of fresh flowers had been taken from a headstone bowl and thrown randomly across the grass. There was no way of knowing which grave they had been taken from, but Michael carefully picked them up and considered the possibilities. His eye fell on the Ratline headstone and he recalled the sad event causing the death of the baby Callum. The ground staff had all felt the tragedy and the mystery of that death. Callum might as well have these flowers and they were replaced in the correct bowl.

When work finished at the police office that Monday afternoon, Fleming made an arrangement to pick up Dougie Campbell at three p.m. sharp from the small slip on the north side of town.

The two men chatted pleasantly while The Marlin chugged at her steady eight knots up the loch. Fleming described the work he had done to make the boat seaworthy and Campbell seemed suitably impressed. His grandfather had owned a boat and the young Douglas Campbell had many pleasant memories from that time.

Fleming went first to his creels and checked each creel in turn, finding small lobsters in two of them. He returned the lobsters to the loch and baited each creel before returning it to the water. The two small lobsters were encouraging but he felt a bit disappointed that the past week had not produced more. Now he set off for the small headland.

He took The Marlin in as close as he dare for the tide was rising and their return by dinghy could be much greater than going ashore. He dropped anchor and took Campbell in the dinghy to the shingle beach where he played out the full length of the painter before tying it off to a tree root above high water mark.

The two of them then set off on the path Fleming had taken on the day of the thunderstorm.

"Everywhere looks the same here." Campbell said in frustration.

He was right though, everywhere seemed to be a repeated picture of pine trunks, pine needles and constant shade from the light of the sun. Fleming stopped.

"This is where I was when I heard the thunder and the woman screaming," he explained. "It was coming from that direction."

They then followed Fleming's suggested direction for about 250 yards before entering a small clearing. In the centre of the clearing was the circle of stones that had formed a fireplace. Only cold ashes occupied it now. Campbell had already noticed the cave.

"Home?" he asked, pointing to it.

"Yes, that's his home. Did you bring your torch, Dougie? I think we will need one."

Both entered the cave and almost immediately needed the light from Campbell's torch. Looking around the limited space they saw the cooking pot Fleming had previously seen. There was a plastic container of fresh water and a pile of dry sticks for firewood. On either side the floor was littered with rabbit skin and bird feathers. At the rear of the cave a 'bed' had been made from soft brush and straw. An old mattress that stunk to the heavens lay across the bed and a crumpled lilac bedspread sat on top of the mattress.

Fleming asked Campbell for his torch in order to search around the bed area. An already nauseous Campbell gave him the torch and watched from where he was as Fleming began his search.

Fleming lifted the mattress, ignoring the soil marks and stains and carefully lit the natural nooks and crannies where wall and floor met. He found a small wooden box, about 8" by 5", and opened it. Inside was a single book, a Bible.

"What is it?" Campbell asked. He could not see into the box from where he was. "Believe it or not, it's a Bible." Fleming said, tilting the box up to show Campbell the closed book in the box. He chose not to tell Campbell that the Bible was a Geneva Bible, very old and probably worth a fair price. "I'll just leave it here."

On the opposite side of the cave they found a fishing rod and reel and several plastic bags filled with crushed clothing. One bag contained the single item of clothing they wanted to find, the green and blue checked heavy shirt.

Campbell got busy with his camera, snapping away at the interior of the cave, the fishing rod, bags of clothing and he took a close-up of the bag with the blue/green shirt.

"We have to take the bag with the shirt, Andy, okay?" Campbell said cautiously.

"Of course, Dougie. I just hope that the owner has not gone for good. The guy had his bike over there by that tree and I don't see it." Fleming said as he began to head out across the clearing in that direction. The bicycle was still there, only now it was lying on its side beneath a plastic sheet and covered with small loose pine branches.

Campbell took more photographs.

"So you were right about the bike all along." Campbell conceded.

"Yeah. If you were to go up that rise and follow the path it would take you out near Mrs MacTaggart's shop," Fleming explained. "After an hour or so."

"You don't want to feel the ashes in the fire and tell me how long they have been gone?" Campbell said sarcastically.

"Unless they put the fire out with their own precious water they have been gone for the weekend." Fleming said confidently.

"And you know this how?"

"The ashes have been damped down. It hasn't rained since Saturday morning."

"Aye right." Campbell said sceptically.

With a final flurry of photography Campbell announced that it was time to go. He had seen enough.

"Wait a minute, Dougie. Give me that torch a second will you?" Fleming asked. "I will put that bed back the way it was."

"They will know that this shirt has gone, Andy. Why bother?"

"Sure, but if everything else looks the same they will suppose that the shirt is their only missing item and they must have misplaced it themselves. I'll put that lilac thing back the way it was. You check around for security cameras." Now it was Fleming's turn to be sarcastic and Campbell nodded and smirked in acknowledgement.

In the cave Fleming took the Bible quickly from the box and stuck it inside his own shirt. The box and the bedding was left exactly as before.

"Right Dougie that's it, we can go now."

Douglas Campbell and the stinking old shirt that was keeping a smile on his face were returned to the north slip. By the time Fleming reached home it was too late to be contacting anyone but after dinner he looked through the old Bible. Someone must know about this old book, printed in Geneva in 1599. He would call Robert Millar in Glasgow. The man had spent his life among books, old and new. He would not be particularly expert in old Bibles but he might well point Fleming towards someone who was.

SIX

Following Robert Millar's advice, Fleming rang Professor Jackson at Edinburgh University. Apparently the professor lectured at St. Andrews University as well and was employed by a leading auction house on matters of ancient documents, manuscripts and rare books.

When Fleming was connected eventually to Professor Jackson he found that she was called Camilla Jackson.

"Camilla Jackson? I am Andrew Fleming, do we know each other?"

"Are you the Andrew Fleming who went to school with me? The same Andrew Fleming who went on a school trip to Hadrian's Wall?"

"That's me, Camilla." Fleming said, a little embarrassed to be speaking, for the first time in twenty years, to the clever girl he had once found so attractive.

He explained that he was now a police officer and that his current enquiries had brought him to be in possession of an old Bible. The book may or may not be required as evidence but what he needed from her was an appraisal of what this old Bible meant historically.

"I would need to see it, Andrew, but it does sound

exciting. We have a very similar item at the National Library here in Edinburgh." the professor told him.

"Does that mean my coming to Edinburgh?" Fleming asked.

"Probably," she answered. "But not necessarily to the university. I could meet you wherever would be convenient for you in the city."

Karen Ratline returned to work feeling fortified by her visit to her parents. As she parked her car in the designated part of the school grounds she found Jean MacIvor watching her from the school door.

"How was your weekend, Karen?" Jean asked, a smile on her face as usual.

"Good." Karen replied. "It was a real tonic and my parents are both well."

"Come through to my office when you are ready, Karen. I have something to go over with you." Jean said in a pleasant tone but until she knew what Jean was talking about Karen felt uneasy. She took her coat to the classroom and took her handbag with her as she quickly walked to Jean's office. They were always first to arrive of the teaching staff and she knew that Jean was making use of this private time together.

With the door closed and both of them seated, Jean MacIvor drew the contents of a large brown envelope out onto her desk. Karen could see that the envelope had 'Head Teacher Only' written in large bold letters.

"These are your medical notes, Karen. They contain information that has not been divulged to me before and I want your side of the story where they are concerned. The Education Authority have supported you following the tragedies in your personal life and want me to comment on your abilities and state of mind after your latest tragedy."

"So that's what this is." Karen said sombrely.

"Yes, that's what it is. There is no request for an inquisition or anything offensive, Karen. They simply want an honest appraisal of how well you are holding up."

"You have read these notes?" Karen asked.

"I have. I know about your breakdown following the death of Callum and the time off you were given for treatment. There are comments in there about your reaction to both deaths in six months as being 'unsurprising'. I would certainly agree with that but what I want to agree with even more is the conclusion of the psychiatrist who reckons that you have regained your mental resilience without bitterness or rancour. Your attitude to children has not suffered from the death of your own child and he found no reason for you not to resume teaching. He suggested a different school and we know that you have transferred."

Jean stopped to look directly at Karen.

"These notes and the full history will not be known to anyone but me unless you choose otherwise, Karen. What they want to hear from me now is how well you are reacting to your recent rape attack. I will be watching and listening to formulate my response."

"I am on some sort of probationary period?" Karen asked with a frown.

"Not as a teacher, Karen, only as a lady who has had more psychological baggage to bear than the rest of us put together. You appear to be doing really well but the effects of trauma can take ages to manifest themselves. I know that from past experience of other teachers. I will respond to this letter today but with a promise of quarterly updates. I hope to have nothing to report but you must be completely honest with me. That is the only way this business can be properly addressed and your own health looked after."

"I feel much better after this past weekend, Jean. I never wanted anyone to know about my breakdown. A lot of people believe that nobody really recovers from these things but I was determined, eventually, that I would fight my way back. I think I have done that."

"I think so too, Karen. Nothing has really changed here. You are doing a great job and that's my current report to you and to the Authority."

Andrew Fleming had arranged to accompany the Procurator Fiscal on one his regular trips to Edinburgh. While the Fiscal went to see his friends at the Crown Office, Fleming would meet Camilla Jackson at the

Waverley Hotel. The Geneva Bible was wrapped in gift paper and a bow, pretending to be a box of chocolates or some other gift (for the purpose of misleading the Fiscal).

Fleming waited in the foyer watching everyone who came and went. Despite the passing of years, he recognised Camilla immediately. She had always walked in her own purposeful way and her style had not changed. For whatever reason, she also recognised him and they smiled at each other in confirmation. They were soon seated, each with coffee paid for by Fleming.

"So, are you going to unwrap your present?" Camilla asked with a pleasant smile.

"This is not a present Camilla, this the property of the Crown, or it soon will be." Fleming said. "What it is lacking, for purposes of reporting to the Procurator Fiscal and the court, is a proper definition of what it is."

Camilla looked first at the cover of the book.

"This is not exactly new, Andy, but in fairly good condition. You say it was in a wooden box. I am guessing that that box may have been made to hide the Bible. Possession of the wrong versions could be like a death warrant at one time. The preacher, Donald Cargill, had a similar means of concealing his Bible."

Fleming was taking notes as she spoke.

She now looked carefully at the book itself and saw the slackening of the binding that had caused the pages to appear loose and misaligned. Camilla put on her reading spectacles as she reached the frontispiece, a highly ornate page with printing confined to a central panel which she read quietly to herself.

"'The Bible and Holy Scriptvres conteyned in the olde and newe Teftament, translated according to the Ebrue and Greke'. Now let's see where, ah here, 'Printed at Geneva by Rouland somebody in M.D.L.X. Now look, Andy, at this address, 'To the moste virtuous and noble queen Elifabeth, Quene of England, France and Ireland etc.Your humble subjects of the Englifh Churche at Geneva, wifh grace and peace from God the Father through Chrift Iefus (sic.) our Lord' "

She gently lifted over the pages, obviously adrift in her own thoughts, she would utter phrases of her observations, "leaf numbering", "Roman texting", "complete Psalms" and "side notes". She turned to Fleming eventually.

"You said this was a covenanter's Bible, Andy. Was that just because of the name Gabriel Ramsay and the date on the front fly page?"

"Yes, mostly the date and the person who currently has possession of it. Apparently she claims covenanting ancestry and apart from this Bible, as far as I know, she owns nothing else of any value whatsoever."

"Mmm." Camilla said with a thoughtful expression. "Let's see what Revelations has to say."

"How is that relevant, Camilla?"

"I doubt that Revelations in this book will differ little from the King James' version, Andy, but the side notes may well be inspired by Calvinist interpretation or Huguenot guidance from Franciscus Junius."

"Who was he?"

"A protestant Huguenot theologian, very anti-catholic. His father was killed by a catholic they say."

She had now reached Revelations and read quietly to herself before holding the book over towards Fleming.

"See the guide notes to Chapter 17, verses 3 and 4? The scarlet coloured beast mentioned in verse 3 is said to be ancient Rome and the woman sitting on it is said to signify 'the new Rome, the Papestrie whose cruelty and bloodshedding is declared by scarlet'. It further claims in the guide notes that 'the woman is the anti-Christ, that is, the Pope with all his filthy creatures'. Sounds very hard-hitting there, don't you think? That would be in keeping with the Presbyterian strength of belief held by the covenanters, though. I think you are quite right about this book, Andy. You are probably correct to think of it as valuable too. The original patent holder for all London printed Bibles and church documents, indeed all government legislation and formal printing was given to Christopher Barker, who died the year before this book was printed in Geneva, and his son Robert Barker who succeeded him, inheriting his patent or privilege rights. This book has been brought back to the UK from Europe."

"Are we talking in thousands here, Camilla?" Andy asked, taken aback.

"I would say so. My interest would be in the history it

represents Andrew. It should be in the National Museum. You will remember that, won't you?"

"Yes, I will. Right now I will have to wrap it up again. I have a plastic bag in my pocket to carry it. I promised the Fiscal that I would be at that junction behind the station at 2.30 exactly, so I had better get moving."

"Let me know how you get on with that Bible, won't you?" Camilla asked in a suggestion of inviting further communication.

"You can count on it, Camilla. You have been a great help, just as I expected; and it has been a pleasure to see you again, just as I expected." Fleming said with an involuntary wink.

As he sat beside the Procurator Fiscal on the return journey Fleming involved himself in the bland conversation on court figures and intended procedural changes, but at the back of his mind was the imperative need to return the Bible to the cave and very quickly thereafter, take action to gain proper legal custody of it. Professor Camilla Jackson had been quite adamant that the book was too precious to be under no particular control.

At the earliest opportunity Fleming drove north to see Mrs MacTaggart. He needed to know if the chap from the cave was active locally, or had he and his mother left the area?

"I heard that they had gone south again, Mr Fleming. One or two locals told me that they had passed them walking south. I am going by the description, mind you, for nobody knows the name of these people. The tall thin chap was wearing a white shirt, or what was once a white shirt."

"Good," said Fleming. "I'll take a look for myself and report back to you, Mrs MacTaggart."

It had long been a tactic of Fleming's to involve genuine witnesses in the spirit of his enquiry. The witness then felt useful and would volunteer information without waiting to be asked. He left the shop and headed off into the woods, the old Bible firmly held within his back pack. Ahead of him lay two hours of walking through fairly dense trees and he was grateful for the shade.

When he reached the clearing he crawled to the same vantage point as before to watch and listen. He considered that both the woman and her son could be present and asleep for all was quiet. The fireplace of stones and ash looked no different and the tell-tale hump of leaves suggested that the bicycle was still hidden under its plastic sheet. He crept stealthily down to the mouth of the cave and listened again. No snoring or audible breathing. It seemed promising but he realised that he should have brought a torch for once he stepped into the shade of the cave all was black. After a minute or so his eyes became more accustomed to the darkness and his previous visit allowed him to find his way to the back of the cave where he knew the old stinking mattress lay. He crawled over it and was delighted to find the empty wooden box. He replaced the Bible and the box lid before returning the box to the place of concealment behind the mattress. From his pocket he took a length of fine fishing gut to create a tell-tale for his next visit.

Satisfied with the success of his mission he left the cave and the sunshine in the clearing almost blinded him. The fresh air more than compensated. He began his walk back in serious thought about what his next steps should be. Dougie Campbell had been wrong to have taken the suspect's blue and green thick shirt away from the cave. It had been the most identifiable feature of the thin man with dark hair. Not only that, he had not been in possession of a warrant. Campbell would argue that the cave did not count as 'premises' but common sense alone made procurement of a warrant a safe procedural step. The last thought was the most relevant to everything they might do. As yet nobody, Fleming included, knew with certainty where this cave lay in terms of jurisdiction. Was it in their own police region, or the one to the north?

He checked in at the village shop and bought a bottle of water.

"They don't seem to be back yet, Mrs MacTaggart. If anything alerts you to their return will you let me know?"

"Of course, Mr Fleming." Mrs MacTaggart replied with the hint of excitement in her voice that told Fleming she was responding to his encouragement.

On the banks of Loch Lomond two young Glasgow

girls were sitting close to a small log fire that seemed to be keeping the midges at bay. The girls were students from the Glasgow School of Art and lived their lives with the gay abandon that allowed them to do whatever felt good at the time. This time it was camping and they had loose ambitions of climbing some mountain or other when they found one they liked. They both wore cut-off denim jeans with brightly coloured tights beneath and they had a selection of various coloured shirts and sleeveless jackets.

Jacki, the taller girl, had a series of metal rings piercing the top outer edge of her right ear, suggesting the absence of a shower curtain and on the left side of her nose was a yellow glass stud that clashed drastically with her peroxide blonde hair, cut short on the left side of her head.

Tania was only slightly shorter but had a noticeably stouter build. Her dark brown hair was longer with bright red highlights and occasional random plaits. She had a single metal ring piercing her right eyebrow and numerous coloured strings of very small beads twisted to form a necklace.

Behind the girls was their tent, a cheap affair and only large enough to house their sleeping bags. A battery powered cassette player provided low level music as they chatted about a rock concert they had attended earlier in the year. They had cans of beer and cigarettes but little food.

Their attention was confined to themselves for the firelight provided no greater view until Tania caught a glimpse of white behind them and let out an involuntary yell. She was attacked immediately by a tall man in a white shirt who simply struck out at her mercilessly before turning his attention to Jacki. He punched Jacki several times about her face and head, causing her to bleed from her nose and right ear. With both girls weakened and groaning the man began to rummage among their possessions. Another female voice broke the night stillness as a woman closer to the road than the camp fire, shouted for someone called 'Mitchell'. The tall man took two tin cans and both girls' purses, before running off towards the calling woman.

The girls had chosen to camp in isolation and had no idea where the nearest assistance could be. They were not so badly injured that they required immediate medical help and decided, for reasons of safety, to remain where they were until first light. They would walk up to the road with what they had left and try to hitch a lift back towards the city.

Chief Inspector Raymond Adam was normally early in reporting for duty. On his arrival at his office that morning he was introduced to Jacki and Tania. The early shift officers had already taken them to the hospital for attention to their wounds and had obtained statements from the doctor on duty to the effect that these wounds were consistent with their accounts of having been assaulted.

Raymond Adam listened carefully to what they had to

say before asking a female sergeant to note their statements individually. This was not a case of serious robbery but it was interesting. Someone wanted their food, their money and responded to an unseen woman calling him 'Mitchell'. This individual must have spent time observing the girls, ensuring that they had no male company, before launching his attack.

Back in Corran Bay, Fleming for once sought the company of Dougie Campbell and they both studied the large ordnance survey map of their police area and beyond.

"I reckon that the cave is in about here." Fleming said, pointing his pen towards a spot in the forested region on the north east shore of the loch. "As we look across to the road, there is the boundary there, but that does not tell us clearly about our jurisdiction. If the easting and northing lines are relevant then the cave is probably just in our area. Do you suppose the Chief Inspector could confirm it? Things would be easier if we can avoid someone else's jurisdiction."

"Two different Sheriffdoms and two different Procurators Fiscal," Campbell thought aloud. "I suppose if we could get them to agree on whose territory that is for their purposes we would be on firmer ground."

"I'll have a word with the Fiscal first, then I'll speak to Mackellar." Campbell decided, surprising Fleming. The Detective Sergeant and Mackellar often appeared to be joined at the hip in opposition to anything Fleming suggested.

"Impress on him the urgency of this, Dougie. We need to retrieve that Bible."

"You're the one who put it back." Campbell said pointedly.

"Yes. It might have been better if you had done the same with the shirt. Having that item without the cover of a warrant is risky."

"We'll manage." Campbell said haughtily, but his face suggested that Fleming's point had been taken.

The Procurators Fiscal reached agreement that the cave's position was so indeterminate that, using the eastings lines as an argument, the cave should be considered to be in the Corran Bay fiscal's territory.

The following morning Fleming and Campbell headed back to the cave armed with a search warrant, again taking The Marlin up the loch for the sake of Campbell's 'bad back'. Fleming felt guilty at the idea of returning to the cave to 'discover' a boxed Bible that he had already found. Campbell felt less guilty about the intended re-discovery of the blue and green shirt.

When they arrived at the clearing in front of the cave Fleming declared himself satisfied that the occupants were not yet in residence.

"How do you know that?" Campbell asked.

"I'll go the mouth of the cave and you keep your eyes on that tree to the left of it."

Fleming walked confidently to the entrance and triggered the fishing line that stretched across it at ankle height. The line pulled away a small stick that held back a branch of the tree. The branch simply swung back to its natural position.

"Fair enough, Crazy Horse." Campbell said as he joined Fleming. "But I am still the guy with the torch."

"Lead on." Fleming invited, knowing that Campbell would walk into the cobwebs before he did. He carefully gathered his fishing line.

The boxed Bible was recovered and Fleming was delighted to have it under judicial control. On the return journey he explained to Campbell just how unique and valuable the book was. He avoided telling him exactly how he knew, beyond research, in case conversation between Campbell and the Procurator Fiscal led to knowledge of his illicit possession on the journey to Edinburgh.

"That book has to have been stolen at some point, Dougie. I just cannot accept that the old spay wife is the legitimate owner."

"Sure, but why would she keep it when she could easily sell it?" Campbell asked.

Fleming had to concede that he had a valid question.

Karen Ratline had lost all the emotional benefit of her weekend at home. The interview with Jean MacIvor on the subject of her mental breakdown had depressed her.

114

The breakdown had not simply happened, like a dose of influenza, it had been caused by events. In her mind, even the subject of the breakdown was a link retrospectively to these events. How could she banish the memories she had if others persisted in raising the subject as if the issues were current? She had been through all this healing and counselling business and it had not been pleasant.

The answer to her sour mood would be the children. They were not in a mood. They lifted one another towards a common interest, a common humour. As the day went on she began to feel their involuntary assistance and her own mood was much improved by mid-afternoon.

Her class had been drawing subjects of their own choosing. Karen would come round when they had finished and try to identify what the subjects had been.

When she came to a young boy called Hastie she knew that he would have drawn animals. He was just crazy about animals.

"These look like animals, Tommy, are they all the same?"

Tommy tapped each figure in turn with his pencil.

"Bunny, bunny, bunny, bunny." he chanted.

Karen gasped. A chill had just run down her back.

At the end of her working day Mary Fleming spoke to her. Mary had noticed her new friend's demeanour and asked Karen what had been bothering her, had it been the talk with Jean?

"Just a bad day all round, Mary. I was so buoyed up

after my weekend and the day has just been a bit flat." Karen explained.

"How do you fancy some baking practice?" Mary asked. "You can come out to my house this evening and we can make some of these adventurous cakes from the cookbook. Hopefully we won't experience 'flat' anymore."

"What about your husband and family?" Karen asked, suggesting that Mary would be neglecting them.

"I have never known Andrew Fleming to bake and the children are past the stage of being interested. We can have the kitchen to ourselves." Mary said enthusiastically.

Karen smiled.

"I would love to, Mary. Seven o'clock, all right?"

Andrew Fleming had returned to the caravan of Jock MacGregor.

"Do you know where the Galloway seer married your friend, Michael?" Jock asked. "I need to know more about this besom's background."

"I never knew about the wedding, Andy, except what Mike told me. They got married in a Registry Office and I have a feeling it was in Strathaven."

"When would that have been, Jock?"

"Fifty-eight or fifty-nine, I would guess." Jock said, his brow furrowed.

"Had Mike any middle names?" Andy asked.

"He was Michael Urquhart Galloway. It's no hard tae see why we a' mind o' that." Jock said with a chuckle.

"Needless to say, he never said much about his middle initial but it aye appeared on his pay packet."

"And she was a Sorbie?" Andrew replied. "Jessie Sorbie."

Jock nodded.

"You'll be off tae check for their wedding particulars next, I suppose." Jock said with a smile. "That's a hell o' a trek."

Andy nodded slowly.

"I need to know what connects Jessie Galloway with Karen Ratline." Andy explained. "Why would Jessie Galloway know about the death of Karen Ratline's baby?"

"Were ye talking to Jessie?" Jock asked with a look of surprise.

"No. She was talking tae herself at the time, Jock, but she knew that a stone had fallen on that wean in his pram. I just overheard her. How would she have known that?"

"She's a witch, Andy. The bitch knows too much for anybody's good." Jock said as if he believed in the woman's alleged powers.

"You never heard where the boy was born? Her own boy, I mean." Andy Fleming asked.

"Not that I remember, Andy. Mike never had much to say about the boy. When he did mention him it was to tell me how backward the boy was, or how his mother never let him out of her sight. I often wondered if the boy was really Mike's bairn. He didnae speak about him the way a father would speak of his son, you know what I mean? He always referred to him as 'the boy', never mentioning him by name. That's why I cannae remember his name."

"So the name Ratline means nothing to you?" Andy asked.

"I never heard of that name until the local paper said that Karen Ratline was the new school teacher's name." Jock said firmly. "It's no the kind of name you hear every day."

"No, it's not. That might be of some help to me." Andy said, rising from his seat beside the door of the caravan. "Oh here, Jock, I nearly forgot tae give ye your biscuits."

Andy Fleming phoned his friend, Billy, a police colleague who happened to stay in Strathaven. He explained to Billy what was needed from his local Registrar and left it with Billy to conduct some enquiry. As Jock McGregor had said, 'it was quite a trek' from Corran Bay to Strathaven.

It was after nine o'clock when Andy got home that evening and he was surprised to find Mary and Karen clearing away a serious number of cooking tins, bowls, packets and utensils. The kitchen table had three large layer cakes and a tray of smaller cupcakes of different types. The children were in bed.

"Who is going to eat that lot?" Andy asked.

"There are plenty of mouths that like cake, Andrew Fleming." Mary said in her mocking tone. "Just because you profess to avoid cake. By the way, this is Karen. I don't think you two have met."

As Karen and Andrew shook hands, Fleming could see the healing marks around Karen's face and the wary look in her eyes.

"Go through and sit down." Mary instructed. "Karen and I will join you shortly with tea and some of the cake you won't want too much of."

Fleming did as he was told with a smile on his face.

When the women joined him, Fleming was content to let them create the flow and topics of conversation. Mary could sense that he was being considerate but also realised how his impatience would be building within him to know more of the lady visitor.

"Andrew is keen to know about your married surname, Karen. Do you know the history of the Ratline family?" Mary asked trying to sound interested.

"I had never heard that name before I met Fraser," Karen said honestly enough. "His family are all in Australia, have been for years, generations even, but he wanted to come back to Britain. He was fairly successful in the insurance company he was with, so that kept him over here, the insurance company and maybe me." she said smiling. "With the exception of his parents, I have not heard of anyone else with that surname."

"What made them go to Australia in the first place?" Fleming asked.

"They were probably deported." Karen said with the

same smile. "His father said the family were once in the military but he did not seem to know or care much about their history. If he knew then he wasn't for telling."

"Oh dear." Andy said as if Karen had just shaken a skeleton in a cupboard. "I hope your own origins are not so mysterious."

"No, not at all. I am just a Thomson from Stonehouse." Karen answered.

"Not too far from the Flemings of Biggar." Andy said, sounding satisfied with her identity. "Good covenanting country." he commented.

Karen Ratline burst into laughter.

"Don't you start, Mr Fleming. My old friend Jennifer Paterson, used to talk about the covenanters as if she knew them all personally."

"Was she studying history or was she somehow connected?" Fleming asked, obviously interested.

"I think we were both connected three hundred years ago but Jennifer's family were seriously keen on keeping the family history alive. Jennifer told me once how mad her mum had been with her for losing an old Bible that had been in the family for years."

"How did she manage to lose it?" Mary asked sympathetically.

"She was taking it to show to the minister when she was delivering his groceries. Someone jumped her and stole the groceries. The man stole the Bible too but he probably didn't realise what it was."

"Was Jennifer hurt in this incident?" Fleming asked.

"Yes, she was hit several times but I think the real pain came when she tried to explain things to her mother. The woman went ballistic, as folks say nowadays."

Fleming was pensive. He imagined an interesting old family Bible inscribed with names and dates of birth, dates of christening, marriages, perhaps.

"How old was this Bible, Karen, did Jennifer tell you?"

"Not really, just that it was a reminder of their past in covenanting times."

"Did you ever see it?"

"No. It was always kept out of sight under lock and key. Jennifer had only seen it once or twice before. I was surprised that she was allowed to take it out of the house to show to the minister."

Andrew Fleming could feel the cold shock of coincidence down his spine.

"Karen, are you still in touch with Jennifer?" he asked.

"I haven't spoken to her since before I got married, but I really should. It is ages since we spoke last."

Fleming smiled and nodded. He looked sideways at Mary and she realised that control of the conversation was being returned to her. Fleming felt that he had a hundred questions he would like to ask Karen Ratline but he had to be careful. Social conversation is quite a different thing to witness interview or interrogation and Karen was intelligent enough to make the distinction.

"You never said whether you liked our cakes." Mary Fleming told him critically.

"To the best of my judgement they were delicious." Fleming said. "Karen is obviously a good cook."

SEVEN

After clearing the enquiry with his local CID boss, Billy Brodie called at the Registrar's Office and laid out what was known about the mother and son thought to be living in a cave in Argyll. The Registrar was interested immediately and told Billy that there would be an old man called Sorbie sitting in the public library 'right now' reading the daily papers. He was probably someone worth speaking to about the Sorbies locally, according the public official.

After a brief enquiry on the computer, the Registrar looked out a large, heavy, leather-bound ledger and began to scan down each page from a certain date. Even with the book upside-down, Billy could admire the handwriting. He had seen old police ledgers and knew that in the days before typewriters and printers, people employed to create records were generally capable of beautiful handwriting. The scrolling finger of the Registrar stopped.

"Fifteenth July 1950, Maxwell Mitchell Sorbie, a son born to Jessie Sorbie, father unknown."

"Does it give any other details, like addresses or relatives?" Billy asked.

"Her address is given as 'c/o Sorbie, Tanhill Farm Cottages. That is also the place of the birth."

"The boy was born at home, was that usual?"

The Registrar adopted a puzzled frown.

"First-borns would normally be at a hospital, even back then, but who knows what the circumstances were?"

"And her marriage to Michael Urquhart Galloway?" Billy asked.

"It came later," the Registrar said closing the ledger and returning it in exchange for another from a lower shelf.

"They were married in 1959. The boy would be about nine years old so I doubt if Galloway was anything but a stepfather to him."

The official laid down the ledger and pursued a systematic search of its contents.

"This looks like it here, Mr Brodie. Michael Urquhart Galloway, forestry worker, to Jessie Sorbie, dairy worker. Her address is still the farm cottages but he is listed as staying at Forest Lodge, Glendaruel, Argyll."

"Does it list anyone else there, her parents or a sibling perhaps?" Billy asked.

"There is a Gwen Sorbie shown as a witness. I think that would be her mother. The same name appears in the birth extract as the reporting witness."

"Thank you very much."

Billy Brodie made his way to the public library and found the old man called Sorbie.

"Aw you mean Maxwell Sorbie, Gwen's man," the man replied to Brodie's enquiry. "He has been dead for years. He was no relative of mine either. I do see Gwen going about still, but we never say much more than 'Hello', in the passing, if you get what I mean."

Billy shrugged and smiled at the old man.

"Thanks anyway."

He called Fleming later and reported what he had learned.

The story around the Ratlines and this Bible of the Patersons' was becoming intriguing but Fleming had to harness his interest. Mackellar had summoned him.

"This is something right down your street," the Chief Inspector said, waving a letter in front of him. "A firm of solicitors in America have been trying to find living relatives of a once-famous movie star but have very little to go on."

"Great," said Fleming. "When do I go?"

Mackellar laughed.

"Oh you don't go to America for this. The living relatives, if they exist, are still in Scotland. All you have to do is find them. There is a local man who once accompanied an elderly couple on a visit to this movie person's ranch. The old folks were related to the lady who has passed away and they were responding to an invitation from her about ten years ago. The man is an Alex Mackenzie and he stays here in Corran Bay. That is why the enquiry has come here. All you have to do is find Alex Mackenzie and learn anything he knows about living relatives of the deceased."

"Why me?" Fleming asked. He knew that this sort of thing was usually a tit-bit for the CID.

"I spoke to Raymond Adam about it earlier today. He suggested yourself."

Mackellar smiled as he spoke, almost inviting Fleming to say something out of place.

"I'll do what I can." was all he said.

On his way downstairs Fleming muttered to himself, "Alex Mackenzie in Corran Bay, like looking for a straw in a haystack".

Four days later Fleming took his own typewritten confidential report to Chief Inspector Mackellar. It showed that Fleming had traced the only living relative of the movie queen. She was a married lady staying in the Morvern peninsula and had never realised that she was the great granddaughter of someone famous and very wealthy.

Mackellar looked genuinely impressed.

"How did you find her?" he asked.

"She is the daughter of an old girlfriend." Fleming said mischievously, making his exit.

As he went downstairs he thought to himself, "Just wait 'til you get the phone bill."

Mary Fleming had invited Karen to the Fleming house for her evening meal on Friday.

"It will be a change from making your own dinner, Karen. One more place at the table will make no difference to me."

Karen Ratline was more relaxed and confident since her all-clear from the doctor. She was also happy to visit Mary and the children. She liked to imagine her little Callum growing up to be like young David Fleming.

Fleming returned home in good spirits after his success with the inheritance enquiry and was pleased to find that Karen Ratline was visiting. After dinner the children went outside for a short time before their bath. It was an opportunity for Fleming to ask his visitor if she had known Jessie Sorbie from Stonehouse.

Karen looked at him with a very serious expression.

"She was witch of a woman." she said firmly, as if Jessie Sorbie could never be a suitable subject for discussion.

"Really?" Fleming said. "Was she regarded as a real witch?"

"Yes she was and for me she can never be anything else." Karen said in the same stern disapproving tone. Jessie Sorbie was apparently a sour subject but Karen obviously knew the woman.

Fleming knew that there was little point in pursuing the matter and changed the subject. Karen Ratline was obviously more comfortable to leave Jessie Sorbie out of their conversation. Fleming privately wondered why. He was disappointed not to hear about Jessie Sorbie from

Karen but he would have to find his answers from somewhere. Douglas Campbell was making no progress in the rape of Karen Ratline and, other than asking his Lanarkshire colleagues to provide what information they could on the robbery of a Bible thirteen years earlier, Campbell had done little towards making progress.

Andrew Fleming was aware that his Lanarkshire friend, Billy Brodie, followed the same shift pattern as himself and would be day-off when he was. Perhaps Billy would agree to meet up with him in Stonehouse and they could pursue enquiry there. It would require the blessing of both their bosses and Fleming did not care to ask Mackellar. He called Raymond Adam and explained what he had in mind.

Detective Superintendent Adam gave no assurance but he would confer with his opposite number in Hamilton and get back to Fleming.

Andrew Fleming then called Billy to make sure he could be free on a day that suited both of them.

There was a light rain falling as Fleming and Brodie entered Stonehouse hoping to find Paterson's Grocery shop. It was still early in the day and the weather was discouraging pedestrians but Fleming spotted an elderly lady who looked as if she might be a local pensioner.

"Excuse me, dear. I am trying to find Paterson's the grocers, can you help me?"

The old lady smiled.

"I thought everyone knew that shop," she said with a chuckle. "It's just the daughter that works there now. She is Jennifer Gilchrist and her shop is just around the corner to the left where that red car is and then first left again."

Fleming thanked the old lady and ran back to the car before she had the chance to resume the conversation.

The two police officers found the shop and realised that it was no longer enjoying the level of trade it had been built to provide. Jennifer Gilchrist, alone in the shop, looked up from a newspaper and recognised the visitors as the police officers she knew to expect that morning.

"Good morning, Jennifer, I am Andrew Fleming and my colleague here is Billy Brodie."

After the handshakes, Fleming explained that they were engaged in a fact-finding exercise in order to better understand their way around a recent rape case in Corran Bay.

"Before you were married, you were Jennifer Paterson, am I right?"

"Yes I was but I have been married to Alan for a good few years now and we have two daughters."

"What does Alan do?"

"He has his own plumbing business and just as well for this shop is not what it was."

"The supermarkets have taken over from local grocers everywhere." Fleming remarked. "There is no personal touch like before."

Jennifer was nodding in agreement.

"Back in the days when you were Jennifer Paterson, you were friends with a girl called Karen Thomson, is that true?" Fleming asked as if he already knew the answer.

Jennifer dropped her head and did not respond immediately.

"We were best friends all through school," she said, before raising her head again. "But we haven't spoken in years."

It was obvious from her behaviour and tone that there was some regrettable reason for her not speaking with Karen.

"What happened Jennifer?" Fleming asked, hoping to sound sympathetic.

Jennifer paused as she considered her answer.

"My mother always had an old Bible, one that had passed down from generation to generation from covenanting times."

She was looking down at her own fingers as she spoke, a gesture that usually accompanied an admission to some form of wrongdoing. Had she looked up she would have seen Fleming's eyes widen in disbelief.

"It is a sore point to talk about. I had the Bible when it was stolen back in 1965. I was taking it to the manse along with the messages from this shop when I got jumped by a young teenage boy who grabbed the cardboard box of groceries I was about to deliver. When I resisted he thumped me on the head but I held on. He punched me again and I went down. He hesitated before running away, as if he wanted to be sure I was all right. Then he took off running, having stolen the messages and the Bible. My mother was livid."

"How did that affect Karen?" Fleming asked.

Jennifer resumed.

"The Bible belonged to my mother and it was always in its own wooden box but I know that when it was stolen it also had the small sheet of folded paper that my mother had told me about so often. The piece of paper was old too and it had a small girl's account of how she had found the book beside the headless bodies of the owner and his son. I don't remember the man's name but it was the name written on the fly-leaf of the Bible. The man and his son had been murdered on the Lockhart Moor by a Captain Lynus Ratline of the King's Dragoons. I will always remember that name."

Jennifer stopped to think how she might continue.

"When Karen and I were still young, we used to talk of the day when we might both be getting married and of how we could be each other's bridesmaid. We were really close back then but after leaving school we were separated by what each of us was doing. I worked for my father, like I said and she was away at university or college, but we remained friends. She was working in Glasgow after that and I would only see her if she came home. I never even knew that she had a boyfriend and she came to me one day and said she was getting married. I was delighted for her, of course and asked her who the lucky man was. She told me that he was an Australian guy called Fraser Ratline. That was only the second time in my whole life I had heard that surname. My reaction was pretty offensive, I must admit, but Karen took it right on the chin and stormed off. I never got invited to her wedding, never mind being asked to be a bridesmaid. She hasn't spoken to me since."

Now she looked squarely at Fleming.

"I know that her husband was killed in a car crash and I wanted to go to her then. I just couldn't. She would think that I was just calling on her because he was out of the way. That would have been wrong but I was afraid of her rejection a second time, you understand."

Jennifer paused again.

"Then there was that awful business with her baby boy. The poor wee soul was only three months old when he died up at the cemetery. After his death Karen went into a deep depression and it was no time for me to interfere. She was seriously ill."

"What was the 'awful business' you mentioned?" Billy asked.

"The top of a tall tombstone fell into his pram and killed him. Karen was visiting her husband's grave at the time." Jennifer said in a sad, disbelieving voice.

Fleming also shook his head.

"Whose tombstone was it?" he asked.

"Well that was talked about a lot at the time because

most local folk believe that nobody was actually buried there. The stone was more like a memorial stone for some famous covenanter called Cameron."

Fleming could scarcely believe what he was hearing but recalled his main reason for having this conversation.

"Jennifer, have you ever heard of a woman called Jessie Sorbie?" he asked.

Now it was Jennifer's turn to be surprised.

"Yes, I have. My mother tells me that she was the woman who once told Karen and me our fortunes by looking at our hands. Took sixpence for doing it, too. Come to think of it she predicted that Karen would see tragedy in her life and I would have two girls."

"Did she live about here?"

"She must have at one time," Jennifer answered. "Her mother still lives here in the village."

"Do you know where she lives?"

"Yes. You want to speak to her don't you?"

As Fleming and Brodie left to find the home of Mrs Sorbie, the rain was still falling in a persistent smirr. Fleming imagined the woman and house he was about to visit. He expected a wizened, mendacious old woman living in a hovel of a home. He had always counselled those younger than himself to 'never assume anything'. It was a day to heed his own advice.

The house was a small single story cottage fronting directly onto the public pavement, just as Jennifer had described. The front door and windows on either side were painted in a deep blue colour and the glass was clean. Fleming knocked.

When the door was opened Fleming felt slightly embarrassed by his own low expectations. Mrs Sorbie was elderly but her clothes were clean and smart, her hair clean and well cared for, her skin and smile suggested an alert and conscientious housewife. Behind her the hall of the small home was neat and tidy.

"Can I help you, gentlemen?" she asked in a kindly way.

"We are both police officers, Mrs Sorbie. I am Andrew Fleming and my colleague is William Brodie. We wondered if we could have a word with you about members of your family. It would help us to understand another enquiry being conducted in the Corran Bay area."

The old lady looked a bit puzzled but her attitude towards police officers had not changed since her mother's time.

"Come in both of you. I will help you all I can but that might not be a lot."

The small front room was well-furnished and Mrs Sorbie obviously kept on top of her housework for nothing was out-of-place or in need of dusting.

"You are a widow, I believe, Mrs Sorbie?"

The old lady simply nodded.

"When exactly did your husband die?"

"He hung himself on 15th August 1950." Mrs Sorbie

said plainly and with no regret in her voice. Fleming noted that this date was precisely one month after Jessie Sorbie had given birth to her son.

"What was your husband's name?"

"Maxwell Sorbie."

"The same name as your daughter's boy." Fleming observed.

"Yes. She calls him Mitchell now though." the old lady said evenly. Fleming noted this.

"What had your husband worked at before he died?" Fleming asked.

"He was just a farm labourer." Gwen Sorbie said as if speaking about someone who had meant little to her.

"Does Jessie, your daughter, still visit here with you?" Fleming asked.

"Yes, she looks by occasionally. She appears out of the blue with that boy of hers. He is about 32 years of age but he never leaves her side when they are here. He has always been retarded, no wonder, the boy never had a chance. They are filthy too, the pair of them. I always make them have a bath and tell them that they can stay for two days. Jessie doesn't mind that all the same. She has always preferred being outside of a house, away in the woods somewhere. She says she feels trapped in a house. I think I can understand that."

"Did she miss her dad?" Fleming pressed. He wanted the answer she was not giving.

Gwen Sorbie looked down at her own hands before lifting her head again and looking earnestly at Fleming.

"My daughter got on very well with her father until she was about 14 years of age and from then on I could see a difference in her. Instead of being a happy playful child she became withdrawn and quiet. She had always played with other children of her own age and could have continued to do that, but they never came around here anymore and she would not go out looking for them. I knew things were not right but would she tell me what was wrong? No. I was left to figure it out for myself. It was in the Spring of 1950 that I noticed her taking sick turns and calling out in her sleep. I wanted the doctor but my husband and Jessie said 'no'. They did not want the doctor. She had just turned 16 years of age and she was determined to leave school as soon as she could. Again her father agreed with her and I began to see what was wrong. Jessie was wearing large clothes, bigger than she should be needing and it was pretty obvious to me that she was pregnant. I asked her who the father of the child was and she maintained that she didn't know his name. I never believed her for a moment. My husband said nothing. He wouldn't speak to her about it, and he wouldn't speak to me about it. I got the doctor to come and he confirmed the pregnancy. She was supposed to be going into hospital for the birth. She had a date for that but was still at home when it was born. The child came early and forceps were used. It was not an easy birth. The doctor and the midwife worked like beavers to keep Jessie and the baby alive."

She paused and shook her head slowly at her own recollection of the time.

"She almost died. So did the boy. It might have been better if they had for neither of them were ever right. I had a difficult daughter to look after and a baby that needed watching round the clock."

"And your husband?" Fleming asked.

"Oh yes, my husband. We had an almighty row because I had registered the boy as Maxwell just to make my point. I accused him of wasting all our lives and told him to leave. Well, he left all right. He went down to the woods and hung himself from a tree. I really didn't want him near me anymore."

"Your husband was the boy's father." Fleming said without making it sound like a question. Gwen Sorbie acknowledged this with a single nod of her head.

"Did the boy ever go to school, Mrs Sorbie?" Brodie asked.

"We tried him at the local primary school but he was causing too much trouble so he couldn't stay there. There were two special schools in the area and he went to both of them for a short time but even then he gave them trouble. He was mentally tied to his mother you see, and she was just like that with him. If they had to be apart against their own will, you could look out, there would be trouble. No, Mitchell was not one for learning. He still can't read or write but he has a photographic memory. If he has once seen a face, a car, a building or travelled a road, he will know it the next time, even if it happens to be years later. When he gets angry and wild he is hard to take and I just remind him of childhood toys and he changes right away, more like a child again. He remembers them you see."

"That must have been hard for you." Brodie observed.

"It was." Mrs Sorbie agreed. "When that boy got old enough he took to stealing things or damaging things and I told Jessie I would not stand for that from anyone in my home. She did not wait to be told twice. One day the pair of them left and that was the last I saw of them for ages."

"When you say that Mitchell stole things, did you know about him stealing the minister's groceries?" Fleming asked.

"Yes. That was when I threw them out. I made a point of going to the Patersons' and paying for these groceries. It was another couple of weeks before Mrs Paterson told me that he had stolen a Bible as well. She refused to take any kind of payment for the Bible."

"Did you ever see the Bible, Mrs Sorbie?" Fleming asked.

"Not really, Mr Fleming. It was in a wooden box and the only thing I saw was that box. Jessie must have been reading it or looking through it though. Once or twice I would catch her putting a book back into the box. I didn't know at that time that it was a Bible. When they left this house the Bible went with them. I did find ... just a minute."

She rose and went to a sideboard drawer. She returned with an envelope. She opened the envelope and gently removed a small sheet of paper.

"I found this on the bedroom floor after they had gone. I have kept it in that drawer for years without mentioning it to anyone. See what you can make of it."

She handed it to Fleming.

The paper was obviously old and frail and Fleming took his time as he opened out the folded sheet. He read aloud, but slowly and hesitantly, as the writing and spelling made comprehension difficult.

"This Bible was found beside the headless bodies of Gabriel Ramsay and his son Daniel on the Lockhart Moor whence they had been murdered by Captain Lynus Ratline of the Kings Dragoons in July 1682. I have promised to take care of this Bible for Mister Ramsay because it was for his faith in this Bible that he died. God rest his soul. Elisabeth Thomson."

Fleming looked up at Mrs Sorbie.

"Mrs Paterson had this Bible." he reminded her.

"She was a Thomson before she married Paterson." Mrs Sorbie said quietly. "I was a Thomson myself before I married but we were not related."

"That explains it." Fleming said.

"It explains more than that," Gwen Sorbie said with some feeling. "It explains my daughter's obsession with the name Ratline. Her head was full of predictions and curses when she left here. It was just part of her illness and I always blamed her father for that, but she kept bringing up the name Ratline and how the Ratlines were all 'damned to Hell', by her way of it. If she had read that piece of paper she would see it as another excuse for her mad ravings."

"Yes, I see," Fleming said thoughtfully. "Have you any desire to keep this piece of paper, Mrs Sorbie? It really belongs with the Bible, you know."

"You are quite right, Mr Fleming. I would have taken it to Mrs Paterson long ago but she has been very cool towards me since that business with Mitchell and the groceries. I was afraid that she would use it to prove that Mitchell attacked her daughter. He did, of course, but he knew nothing about the Bible. He just hasn't the wits for it. He wanted the food and I was threatening to put them both out of here at the time."

"So you have no objection to my re-uniting this with the Bible?"

"You have the Bible?" Gwen Sorbie asked.

"Not personally," Fleming said. "But I do know where it is. It is safe."

"That is wonderful, Mr Fleming. I am really pleased to hear that and I am glad for Mrs Paterson too. This little village of ours has had its fair share of covenanters, you know. The Sorbies and the Thomsons were aye owners of the covenant and folks about here are not ashamed of their heritage. You saw the cemetery off Manse Road? Well, that was the site of the original St. Ninians Church. James Renwick, the covenanter preacher, preached in that kirk on Sunday the 17th January 1686. It was the only time that he used a kirk to preach after turning to the covenant."

"The kirk would be full, that Sunday, Mrs Sorbie." Fleming said with a smile.

"I believe it was, Mr Fleming. Standing room only as they say and that was four years after that declaration you are holding."

"Has your daughter been here recently?" Fleming asked.

"She was here the week before last. They stayed for two days. They were stinking as usual and I only gave them two days before telling them to go. The place got a thorough clean once they had gone I can tell you."

"I might as well speak to Mrs Paterson while I am in Stonehouse. Do you know her address, Mrs Sorbie?"

Gwen Sorbie laughed.

"It is at the end of the street, Mr Fleming," she said, pointing the direction. "A white bungalow set back from the road. Old Bob Paterson was one of the wealthiest men in Stonehouse at one time. That was when he built that house."

"I think we can find it." Fleming said confidently. "Thanks for being such a help."

As the two men left to walk down the street, Brodie had a question.

"What's all this 'owner' of the covenant?"

"It was how things were said back in the days of the covenanters" Fleming replied. "Do you remember when you were young and your folks suspected you of doing something wrong? They would encourage you to own up? That meant they wanted you to be free and honest about it. The covenanters were so adherent to their faith that they made no secret of their beliefs, even when admitting it would cost them their life."

"Right." said Billy.

"Did you notice how Gwen Sorbie always referred to Mrs Paterson as 'Mrs Paterson' and not by any familiar name?" Fleming asked his colleague.

"Yes, I did."

"That belongs to a bygone age as well. The well-to-do were often referred to as 'Mrs' or 'Mr' rather than use their first names. It was disrespectful to assume the person's consent, or so they thought."

"Just because they had a few bob?" Billy asked.

"Just because they had a good few bob more than common folks like you and me Billy."

"My folks had a shop, Andy."

"Oh sorry, Mr Brodie."

They reached the bungalow described by Gwen Sorbie. It was old, like all the houses, but still looked unique in design. The garden was immaculately maintained.

When his knock on the cut-glass front door was answered, Fleming saw a smart looking elderly lady with her hair in place and her clothing of obvious quality. Her bright eyes suggested an alert mind. Her enquiring 'Yes?' was followed by a quick smile.

Fleming introduced himself and Billy Brodie and explained that they were attempting to patch together the pieces of information from previous years with a view to understanding a serious crime that had happened more recently.

"Oh that sounds mighty involved." Mrs Paterson said with a puzzled look on her face.

"Would it help to mention to you a missing Bible once owned by a covenanter?" Fleming asked, hoping for the invitation that was not yet forthcoming.

Mrs Paterson drew both of her hands up to meet the sides of her face.

"Not Ramsay's Bible?" she exclaimed.

"Gabriel Ramsay." Fleming said quietly.

"Oh come in, gentlemen." Mrs Paterson said, retreating at pace into her own front lounge, her eagerness all too evident. Billy Brodie closed the front door behind them. "Sit down, please."

The two officers sat on a long settee and sank a little into the cushions.

"Is Mr Paterson still with you?" Fleming asked.

"No, Bob passed two years ago." his host said softly.

"Sorry to hear that, Mrs Paterson, but it does mean that we are quite properly speaking about your own interest here without excluding your husband from the

143

conversation. Am I right in thinking that the matter of the covenanter's Bible was a Thomson family undertaking; an honouring of a promise made long ago by one Elisabeth Thomson?"

"Yes that is true, Mr Fleming. Because of marriages, the keeper of the Bible has usually been a woman of a different name but it has always been a Thomson girl. I was Annabelle Thomson before I married Bob. I would have hoped that I could pass the Bible on to my daughter Jennifer. She is Mrs Gilchrist now."

"Yes, we have met Jennifer, Mrs Paterson."

"Oh." she said, as if surprised at not having heard by now.

"Just this morning. We have also met Mrs Sorbie." Fleming said as he looked at Mrs Paterson's face for her reaction.

The lady's face remained the same but it was raised slightly as if to escape a subject beneath her. Fleming continued.

"Mrs Sorbie has been helpful to us and ultimately, I expect, to you. I do not have a Bible to show you this morning, Mrs Paterson, but I do have a Bible. Please describe to me, in as much detail as you can, the Bible you had been keeping in the Thomson family?"

"Well, it was always in a tight-fitting wooden box. That box was specially made for Elisabeth Thomson by the man she married, a carpenter called Daniel Sorbie."

Fleming nodded but said nothing.

"The front of the Bible had an inscription to say that it belonged to Gabriel Ramsay and openly declared that he was a follower of the covenant." Mrs Paterson said as if there was no more to be said.

"You are describing a book you have seen, Mrs Paterson." Fleming conceded. "Did you ever read the book or find anything by which you could describe it further?"

Mrs Paterson fell silent and looked up at her ceiling as if considering the question.

"There was always a small, folded sheet of paper kept inside the pages of the Bible. It had been written in her own blood by young Elisabeth Thomson and told of how she had found the Bible beside the bodies of the two Ramsays, father and son. They had been beheaded by a Captain Ratline of the King's Dragoons. It does not say anything in that note about Lynus Ratline stealing the Ramsay Mill, but folks about here know that he did. The place is a ruin now and nobody would touch it. They say that the Ratline name was cursed by the covenanters of the day and I am afraid that people in this area have long memories. Young Elisabeth Thomson spoke for all of us when she wrote her 'blood oath' declaration."

"Is that why Karen Thomson was ostracised when she married Fraser Ratline?" Fleming asked.

"I don't think anyone wanted to ostracise Karen but she should have known better than to marry someone of that name in a place like this." Mrs Paterson said with indignation.

"Did anyone consider it possible that Fraser Ratline was not someone of the same character as Lynus Ratline?" Fleming asked.

"I think that Karen Thomson knew the history of the Ratline name the same as the rest of us." Mrs Paterson argued. "It was her decision and she paid for it."

"Yes, she paid quite heavily in fact." Fleming said as if to remind Mrs Paterson that Karen Thomson's feelings were due to be considered as much as hers.

"Nobody wanted what happened." Mrs Paterson said, hoping to excuse herself. "Nobody knew the man and nobody would ever wish for the death of a baby."

"Getting back to the matter of the Bible, Mrs Paterson, what would your attitude be, if I was to suggest to you that the Geneva Bible and the sheet of paper inside it should be in the possession of the National Museum for Scotland?" Fleming asked without emphasis.

"It does not belong to them." Mrs Paterson said with some pique. "It belongs to the Thomson family and their descendants. It has done for generations."

"Yes, I know, Mrs Paterson, but I believe the museum could preserve it better than any domestic surroundings and it has been stolen once already. The museum having it for display does not necessarily mean that you would lose ownership, either. I can put you in touch with someone who can describe the options better than I can. I just think that as time passes your practice of holding onto this Bible domestically is denying the Scottish public the opportunity to grasp the true significance of it."

Mrs Paterson looked thoughtful again.

"You have the Bible somewhere?"

"Yes," replied Fleming. "I have it in safekeeping for the moment. It is actually evidence in the case I am working on, and so is this."

He drew the small cellophane envelope from his pocket and allowed Mrs Paterson to see that it contained Elisabeth Thomson's declaration.

Mrs Paterson repeated her initial reaction of placing her hands to her face.

"When the case has been disposed at court, then these items, the Bible and this declaration, will be returned. I would ask you to consider the option of the National Museum. There would be no harm in discussing the matter with Professor Jackson."

"I will give it some thought, Mr Fleming. I have two granddaughters who could accept responsibility for the Bible."

"At some point someone will make a decision on their willingness to adopt that responsibility." Fleming stated.

"On another topic; concerning the robbery of the groceries and the Bible, do you still harbour ill-feelings towards Mrs Gwen Sorbie?"

Mrs Paterson opened her eyes wide in surprise at the question but did not answer immediately.

147

"The whole village knows who stole the Bible, Mr Fleming. It was that crazy grandson of hers, Mitchell Sorbie. He and his mother took off as soon as it happened."

"That was not the question, Mrs Paterson," Fleming reminded her gently. "Mrs Gwen Sorbie?"

Mrs Paterson looked wounded and rubbed her hands together as if she felt uneasy at being asked.

"I am not sure how to feel about Gwen. We still speak, you know, I always say 'Hello' but no more than that. I suppose that is what you mean. She is not to blame for what happened and she would prefer never to have clapped eyes on that husband of hers. He ruined her life."

"And yet he was a Sorbie." Fleming said as if debating the worth of a surname, be it Ratline or Sorbie.

The point was not lost on Annabelle Paterson.

"Were there no black sheep among the Flemings?" she asked.

"Of course," Andy said with a smile. "But like yourself, I prefer to forget them and remember the likes of old Tom Fleming. He died at the Battle of Drumclog in 1679."

"All right, all right," Mrs Paterson responded. "So all Ratlines may not be same and you think I should resume diplomatic relations with Gwen Sorbie?"

"You have Gwen to thank for the recovery of Elisabeth Thomson's declaration." Fleming said. "And I suspect that the woman has never done anything, or even felt anything, to deserve your rejection. The blame lies elsewhere, as you know, but I leave the matter with you."

Mrs Paterson relaxed visibly as she realised that her haughtiness was unbecoming. With some effort, she produced a smile.

"I believe Karen is up in your part of the world these days, Mr Fleming. How is she keeping?" Mrs Paterson asked, clasping her hands on top of her knees and sounding a touch more civilised.

"She is still in the process of recovering, Mrs Paterson, but she seems to be a strong lady and a first rate teacher. Her cooking is to be commended too."

EIGHT

Fleming had considered visiting Karen Ratline's mother but decided against it as he had not yet won Karen's confidence. It was true that Karen and Mary had struck up a genuine friendship but he was not prepared to risk the wrath of both women by pressing Karen or her mother for answers.

When he returned to Corran Bay, he telephoned Raymond Adam and gave him a resumé of what he had learned from those he had met in Stonehouse.

"So in terms of evidence, you have a 300 years old declaration written in blood that ties this Sorbie woman to a Bible theft in Lanarkshire eighteen years ago?" Adam said.

"That's true, sir, but I am also hearing the tone of voice being used by the people behind the history of that theft." Fleming said, deliberately sounding more satisfied than the Detective Chief Inspector was suggesting he should be.

"So, what does that give you, beyond your fur and feathers?" Adam said coldly.

"It gives me cement for my shoogly dyke." Fleming said firmly. "Look at this attack and rape on Karen Ratline. Why was the culprit there? How did he know her name? It was beginning to get dark at the time it happened, yet he recognised her. Why attack her at all? There has been no other similar rape in the whole area to attribute to this man, a man that we don't know yet. There was no attempt to steal her car. There was no attempt to steal her purse. Could she really be unfortunate enough as to meet a sex-mad fisherman with no driving ability in the middle of nowhere?"

"That's why Mr Campbell has got nowhere with it, Andy. It is a problem case."

"But it happened, sir. There had to be motivation and the extent of violence makes it seem personal."

"So Karen Ratline was targeted, you think?" Adam asked more patiently.

"I think the perpetrator has a hatred for Karen Ratline. I think he is someone possessed of a narrow prejudiced mind and to understand this attack we have to broaden our own minds to allow for his unusual and twisted motivation."

"All right, Andy. I can't fault your thinking but you are still at the fur and feathers stage, right?"

"Right, sir."

"This Sorbie character and his mother are still on the loose somewhere, right?"

"Right again, sir."

"Will you know if they return to your area?"

"I would expect to hear about it," Fleming said. "But I will also go searching if there is no word."

When he returned home Fleming saw a small mini car in front of his house. It was fairly conspicuous due to stickers placed side-by-side on the front of the bonnet. They were a pair of 'Audrey Hepburn' eyes from 'Breakfast at Tiffany's' and would attract anyone's attention. Fleming had seen the mini before in traffic around town but only recently had he realised that the owner was Karen Ratline. He chuckled to himself as he drove into his driveway but a more sobering thought occurred to him. Mitchell Sorbie had been described by his grandmother as having a photographic memory. Karen had owned this mini for five years. It would have been parked outside her parents' home on many occasions and Mitchell Sorbie must have seen it and known to whom it belonged.

"Hello Karen. How did I guess that the mini could be your car?" he asked in good humour when he entered the kitchen and found Mary and Karen in the midst of some baking.

"Everyone knows that car." Karen said with a smile.

"That's what I thought." Andy replied. "You've had it from new, right?"

Mary drew him a disapproving look.

"Yes. I don't remember which I saw first, the car or the 'eyes' but it just had to be my car, so I bought it. I still like it." Karen continued without suspicion. She was accustomed to her car being the subject of inquisitive conversation.

Fleming laughed and went through to the lounge where the children were playing a board game. He caught up with the latest football news from the newspaper and waited for dinner to be ready.

After dinner Karen and Mary washed up the dishes and joined Andy in the lounge.

"I was down in your old neck-of-the-woods today, Karen." Fleming said. "I have a good friend down there and we were in Stonehouse at one point."

"You never saw my parents?" Karen said in a way that made Fleming wonder if she would have wanted him to meet them or not.

"No. I don't know where they stay." Fleming said, suggesting that any meeting could only have been a social call.

"Did you stop at all?" Karen asked.

"I was at a shop." Fleming said, purposefully vague.

"You weren't at the cemetery?" Karen asked, again making Fleming wonder what kind of answer she wanted.

"No. I don't really know Stonehouse, Karen. Perhaps we can go there with you someday; someday when you feel like speaking about the past and pointing out the places that matter to you."

"Perhaps, Andy. I pray for such a day and I am working on it."

"Just let me know when you are ready."

On his return to work the following morning Andrew

Fleming received a call from Mrs MacTaggart of the village shop six miles north of Corran Bay.

"I think they are back, Mister Fleming. Ewan lost two loaves from his van this morning. He was early, too early for me, but when he came back out from by back store he found two loaves missing from one of his bread boards. You know that only that character with the bike is on the go as early as that." Mrs MacTaggart reported with some passion.

"But Ewan never actually saw him, is that the case, Mrs MacTaggart?" Fleming asked.

"No. He said that to me himself. He had double checked my own order and that delayed him enough to miss seeing the thief." the shopkeeper agreed.

"All right, Mrs MacTaggart. I believe you when you say it probably was that same man, but let me know of any sightings of him, just to be sure." Fleming said in as kindly a tone as he could.

"I will, of course, Mister Fleming."

As Fleming put the phone down Douglas Campbell came into the room.

"How did you get on down in Lanarkshire, Andy? I heard you were foraging about for answers."

"Yeah. I was filling in the background to the old Bible we took from the cave, Dougie. That book is worth a fortune apparently but should really be in the National Museum. It is at least 300 years old and, until it was stolen about 18 years ago, was in the safekeeping of the Thomson family in the Stonehouse area." Fleming explained, aware that Raymond Adam had probably told Campbell all this already.

"So what is that old bitch doing with it?" Campbell asked.

"Well she isn't trying to sell it so she may not know that it is worth a good price. What she does know, I suspect, is that her son stole the book in the first place and she is keeping it to ensure that it is never found by anyone who would connect her son to the original theft. In fact the theft was a robbery as far as I can gather. The delivery girl was attacked and robbed of groceries as well as the Bible by a tall thin dark haired teenager."

"Wonder where they are now?" Campbell said without hope of a reply.

"They may be back at that cave, according to Mrs MacTaggart. That was her on the phone. The bread man lost more bread this morning but he never actually saw the thief." Fleming told him.

"We can get the son for stealing a Bible eighteen years ago in Lanarkshire but not for raping and almost killing a schoolteacher in our area this summer." Campbell said with disgust.

Fleming simply smiled at him. When things were more positive Detective Sergeant Campbell would not be referring to 'we' as those involved.

"You speak for yourself, Mister Campbell. I intend to catch Mitchell Sorbie and have him convicted." Fleming said with confidence. "When I am confident that Sorbie and his mother have returned to the cave, I intend to go there and apprehend him.

"For what?"

Fleming shrugged his shoulders.

"Theft or reset of a Bible."

Fleming did not have to wait long for the confidence he wanted. Mrs MacTaggart phoned again about lunchtime.

"They are definitely back, Mister Fleming." she announced excitedly. Old Sandy Grant up at Ghennaville chased a young man stealing his hens this morning. A tall thin man with long black hair and flappy trousers."

"Sounds like our man, right enough, Mrs MacTaggart. Did he catch him?"

"No and he never reported it to the police either, Mister Fleming, for he fired a shotgun after the chap and he isnae wanting tae be telling that to the police. Two good browns the man took; took them alive too."

"They will lay more eggs in that condition, Mrs MacTaggart." Fleming said a little cheekily. "Thank you very much, my dear, now I am sure the Sorbies are back."

He told Raymond Adam by telephone of what had just been reported to him and of how he intended to move in for Sorbie.

"Why now?" Adam asked.

"Because there is a case against him for robbery in Lanarkshire eighteen years ago; there is a suspicion of theft of hens this morning; there is a possibility that in that theft of the hens this morning he may have been injured; he is the prime suspect for the rape and attempted murder of Karen Ratline and the calendar is working against us in credibility terms."

"Wait for me, Andy. I am coming up there. I will call Lanarkshire and let them know what we are doing but wait 'til I can join you before doing anything about Sorbie. Have you spoken to Dougie Campbell?"

"Dougie knows all that I have just told you, sir." Fleming said, his voice betraying the reluctance he had felt in keeping Campbell in the loop.

Fleming wanted to visit old Jock MacGregor, but Adam would arrive in an hour's time and Andrew Fleming hated having to watch the clock where friends were concerned. He went, instead, to the furniture store behind the office to see if he could procure a cardboard box large enough to house two brown hens comfortably.

Mindful of the fact that a woman was involved in a situation where searching or controlling of that woman might be required, Adam brought two experienced women police officers with him. Campbell had arranged a further search warrant in respect of the cave and the three men and two women officers set off in two vehicles to seek the Sorbies.

The cars were parked outside Mrs MacTaggart's shop. Before leading his colleagues into the forest, Fleming went in to tell Mrs MacTaggart what was happening.

After walking for an hour and listening to impatient comments on how far this walk was becoming, Fleming signalled the others to stop.

"Just ahead of us here, the path goes off to the left but by walking dead ahead we can place ourselves on a higher piece of ground with the cave beneath us. I have been here often and it provides a vantage point to see what they are doing without being seen by them."

Adam nodded in agreement.

"We must be quiet though." Fleming warned as he turned and led them slowly over a carpet of pine needles and grass until they could all look down on the clearing below. A small log fire was burning in the circle of stones. On the far side of the fire a brown hen with a seriously clipped wing was tied by a long narrow rope to the frame of Mitchell Sorbie's bicycle. The mother and son could not be seen but their voices could be heard within the cave, too soft for the officers to make out anything that the couple were saying. Fleming nodded to his colleagues to follow him back to the path where they walked carefully around to the clearing and approached the opening of the cave.

From within the cave came the shouting that Fleming had heard previously. It was Mitchell Sorbie's voice calling out in triumphant tones "Bunny, bunny, bunny," the word kept repeating and the police officers entered the cave with lit torches.

On the dirty old mattress at the back of the cave was

Mitchell Sorbie, lying on top of his mother, Jessie. Both were completely naked and engaged in sexual intercourse.

Jessie Sorbie was first to react to the torchlight and struggled to remove herself from beneath her son. Mitchell, for his part, chose to be oblivious to the torchlight and obviously wished to continue. He caught his mother by her hair and attempted to return her to her former position, screaming at her, "Bunny, more bunny."

"No Mitchell." Jessie replied angrily. "Let me get my clothes."

Only now did Mitchell seem to realise that something was wrong. He turned to face into the torchlight. "Who's that?" he asked, his voice almost childlike.

"We are police officers." Raymond Adam announced. "We have a warrant to search this cave for items you are suspected of stealing."

"Stealing what?" Jessie asked, her voice showing her deep resentment at the interruption. By now she had struggled into her dress. Mitchell Sorbie was donning his wide legged trousers.

"Two brown hens from this morning," Adam replied. "One is pecking away outside but where is the other one?"

Jessie moved quickly to the side of the cave and, reaching into the darkness, pulled out a handful of loose feathers that she threw into the air.

"That's the other one." she said, her crazed eyes flashing with delight. Mitchell Sorbie sniggered. When

Campbell moved to gather the feathers into a polythene bag, Mitchell sniggered even more. He failed to see why anyone would want the feathers.

"Anything else?" Jessie asked cheekily.

"Yes. A Bible that your son stole from a delivery girl eighteen years ago near Stonehouse." Adam declared with confidence.

"You're no getting my Bible," Jessie rasped as she instinctively backed towards the far end of the cave where the boxed Bible had once been hidden. She turned and threw herself across the filthy mattress. Beyond the mattress she frantically searched with both hands in the dark recess beneath the back wall of the cave.

"Where is it?" she screamed, her wild eyes showing anger that made the officers wary of her next move.

"Oh, we already have the Bible, Miss Sorbie," Adam told her. "You have had it for far too long, certainly long enough to have read the eighteenth chapter of Leviticus."

Jessie looked at him and the other smiling officers in turn.

"What does that mean?" she asked.

"It means that you and your son having sex is committing the crime of incest. The eighteenth chapter of Leviticus lists the close relationships by which incest is defined." Adam said solemnly.

Jessie momentarily looked as if she had another mouthful of protest but chose to say nothing.

"Matters do not stop there, Miss Sorbie," Adam

resumed. "Your son here is suspected of attacking and raping a young school teacher.."

He was not allowed to continue for Jessie Sorbie came to life again and made a lunge for her son. The two female officers caught hold of her and fought to restrain her. This did not stop Jessie's high pitched abuse of her son.

"You ill-begotten bastard," she screamed. "You were told to kill her, not rape her."

Adam, Campbell and Fleming had been prepared for an attack on them by Mitchell Sorbie but the behaviour of his mother was scaring Mitchell and he turned and fled from the cave. Fleming set off in pursuit, aware that his colleagues were not able.

As he quickly lost ground in the chase Fleming realised that Mitchell Sorbie had inherited many of the athletic attributes of the man he had been named after. The guy could run.

The original Mitchell Sorbie had been a winner of the Red Hose Race at Carnwath, a traditional annual three mile race run over the Lands of Carnwath since 1508. The original purpose had been to identify the region's fastest runner and present him with a pair of red hose (socks). This athlete, identified by the long red socks, could then serve to bring or deliver news of travelling armies. The same Mitchell Sorbie had won the Short Run, the Long Run and the Steeplechase at Leith Gymnastic Games in 1850.

Fleming felt as if he was pursuing a ghost for he lost

sight of Mitchell Sorbie. His pursuit slowed to a tracking exercise with disturbed leaves and pine needles confirming the route taken by the running man. Eventually the tell-tale signs ceased. Mitchell Sorbie had evidently taken to the rocky surfaces now appearing on the left of the trail. Fleming climbed over the rocks and saw a distinct pathway of bare earth leading through the trees. Which way now?

Andrew Fleming recalled the path leading north away from the crime scene of Karen's rape and imagined that by turning right he would be headed in that direction. To turn left would lead him back towards the path from the cave to the shop. Sorbie would have gone to the right, Fleming felt certain and he began to run in that direction.

A few minutes later he arrived at the layby close to the water's edge just as he had forecast. The same puddle ran across the path just north of the layby and Fleming was encouraged to see that the muddy water had recently been splashed over the edges of the path. In the layby there was no sign of Sorbie. Had he hidden a second bicycle here? Fleming pushed through the undergrowth on the south side of the layby where Karen had been raped. The grass was now upright but a division had been made by someone passing through it.

Andrew Fleming picked his way through the thick grass in a diagonal line towards the sea. Ahead of him he heard a heavy rock fall and knew that Sorbie had to be near. When he breached the last of the long grass he found only bare rocks and a shallow shingle beach. Sorbie was not visible but he had to be hidden somehow. Fleming returned to the edge of the rocks and began to tread warily over them. He would expect these large rocks to be steadfastly rooted in the sand and shingle and most could be trusted to remain solid. Then he found an exception.

A large slab of rock lying upright against others was unsteady. The lichen and moss did not bridge the rocks as it did elsewhere. Fleming pushed the slab with his foot and it fell away exposing an entrance hole beneath the rocks on which he was standing. Another cave of sorts, enough to conceal his quarry Fleming felt sure. He jumped down in front of the hole and almost immediately the wild crazed figure of Mitchell Sorbie was upon him. Fleming felt Sorbie's hands spread around his throat. The rush of his assailant had caught Fleming off balance and he had fallen backwards onto the thick slab he had just dislodged. Now Sorbie was using his grip of the policeman's throat to repeatedly strike the rock with Fleming's head in exactly the same manner as he done with Karen Ratline. But Andrew Fleming was not Karen Ratline and with both hands free the advantage Sorbie currently had over him would not last. Fleming drove both his fists upwards between Sorbie's arms and forced them apart, loosening the grip of Mitchell Sorbie's hands.

The two men struggled among the rocks with Sorbie engaging the animal tactics of biting and butting. For Fleming's part, he knew that he would have to return Sorbie to the custody of his colleagues and would much prefer to walk him there. Unconsciousness and broken limbs were not an option. Finally he managed to twist Sorbie's arm into a tight lock with the younger man face down in the shingle. Sorbie relaxed in the way a beaten man does and Fleming secured both wrists in handcuffs.

Both lay panting for a few moments without speaking or moving. Fleming was the first to rise from the ground. Looking across at the small cave he could see that it contained a quilted item in a shiny mauve colour. It was easy to imagine Mitchell spending time in that hole with something warm around him. Mitchell Sorbie began to get to his feet and Fleming's attention was immediately drawn back to ensuring that no further running could take place. He gripped Sorbie by his naked arm and led him back through the grass, pausing briefly at the rape site, Fleming remarked, "This is where you raped Karen, didn't you? Damned near killed her too."

"How do you know about me?" Mitchell Sorbie said like a child trying to avoid accusation.

Fleming reached into his pocket and took out the cycle clip he had been carrying since his visit to the crime scene weeks earlier. He showed it to Sorbie and awaited a reaction.

"It wasn't me. I just lost it. I never killed him." Sorbie said in an obvious and clumsy lie, a lie that puzzled Fleming.

"What do you mean 'I never killed him'? Karen is a woman. What the hell are you talking about, man?"

Sorbie said nothing. He frowned in a puzzled, confused way that had Fleming reminding himself that this chap was mentally disturbed. He returned the cycle clip to his pocket and continued to march Sorbie northwards along the dirt path.

Raymond Adam and Douglas Campbell meantime had completed their search of the cave under Jessie Sorbie's constant verbal barrage of expletive abuse. Nothing incriminating was found within the cave but there was the matter of the harnessed hen in the 'yard'. Campbell was told to place it in the cardboard box that Fleming had so thoughtfully brought to the party. The group then began to retrace their steps along the path to Mrs MacTaggart's shop with Jessie violently resisting the idea every inch of the way. She was handcuffed but that did not stop her kicking out, spitting, stopping or pulling the female officers this way and that as they went. Even so, the most offensive feature from Jessie was her body odour. Adam and Campbell kept their distance.

Where the two paths converged and became one, the Adam group could see the approaching Fleming with his captive, Mitchell Sorbie. Fleming gripped Mitchell more securely in case the sight of his mother might encourage him to take flight again.

"So you can run too, Fleming." Raymond Adam remarked as the pair came close.

"Not as fast as this man, I can tell you." Fleming countered. "I just got lucky in the ambush."

Adam laughed and nodded.

"I am the only one here without a prisoner." Adam commented, nodding backwards towards Campbell who was struggling to keep the hen beneath the lid of the box.

They all duly arrived at the shop and divided their numbers so that Adam took Jessie and her escorts with him while Campbell drove Mitchell, Fleming and the brown hen. As the cars drove away, a timid Mrs MacTaggart opened the shop door just enough to watch them go.

Adam and Campbell were finding it difficult to open their car windows sufficiently.

On their return to the police office the CID officers took over the custody of the Sorbies and arranged for separate clinical examination of each. Fleming phoned Mrs MacTaggart for the name and telephone number of the farmer who had lost his two brown hens that morning. The farmer came and identified his surviving hen and the feathers remaining from the other. With the animal photographed he was allowed to take it home against signature. Mitchell Sorbie was not injured and no mention was ever made of a shotgun.

With nothing further to do in the case for the moment, Fleming called Willie Brodie in Lanarkshire and brought him up-to-speed with events. He was still blethering to

Willie when Hamish MacLeod came into the room, eager to hear what had happened at the cave.

When Fleming had recounted the story to his friend in Lanarkshire, he began over again for Hamish's benefit. Then he remembered someone else he wanted to brief on recent events and set off for the caravan encampment on the edge of town.

Big Jock MacGregor's van was closed and locked. Fleming was uneasy about this. Over the past two years he had never failed to find Jock at home when he called. Behind him he heard someone call out, "Andy". It was Maggie McPhee. The old lady was scurrying across the short grass as fast as she could.

"Jock's been ta'en tae hospital, Andy. He wisnae that great on Sunday and an ambulance was sent for. He's up in the County Hospital but he is a bit better, I saw him yesterday."

"I'll just head up there just now, Maggie. Thanks for letting me know."

Fleming found Jock MacGregor sitting up in bed at the hospital with an oxygen feed to his nostrils. The old man smiled when he saw Andy coming in.

"I wondered how long it would take ye to find me." he said with a smile.

"Maggie kept me right." Andy informed him. "Are ye better than Sunday?"

"Brand new, Andy. I could really get used to this place.

The meals are no as bad as folk say and the craic is pretty good tae. Did ye bring they biscuits?"

"I have them here," said Fleming, drawing the packet from a polythene bag.

"I have my two in custody, Jock," he said as he placed the biscuits on top of Jock's bedside cabinet. "Jessie and Mitchell Sorbie."

"That's the name," Jock exclaimed, slapping his leg through the bedclothes. "The boy was Mitchell. Are they locked up?"

"Aye. The mother stole a valuable Bible in Stonehouse eighteen years ago and Mitchell is the guy that attacked and raped the schoolteacher." Andy confirmed, choosing for the moment not to confirm Jock's long held belief of the couple's incestuous relationship.

"So you have all your answers now, Officer Fleming." Jock said with mock formality.

"Not really, Jock, there are answers enough to fit the charges but some things still puzzle me."

"What kind of things?" Jock asked.

"Well as far as I can make out Jessie and Mitchell Sorbie are not known to social services and are not in receipt of any benefits from the welfare system."

"So how have they got by?" Jock interrupted. "Well I doubt that they are doing all right now but they were well enough off after Mike Galloway died."

"Life insurance?"

"Aye, a hefty life insurance. Mike was working at

Cruachan like I told you and earning good money but we all know how these things don't last. Mike took out a policy to cover his own death and pay the sum into a trust for the wife and her boy. The idea of the trust was that the wife, Jessie, would be entitled tae so much every month and no more until the funds ran out."

"So Michael must have made a will." Fleming said.

"He did." Jock said emphatically. "I mind o' that for I went with him. He got the top lawyer in Corran Bay to set it all up for him; the will; the trust; everything just like Mike wanted it."

"Who was the solicitor?" Fleming asked.

"It was that bloke that died a couple of months ago, Gordon something or other." Jock said, a little annoyed at himself for failing to recall the surname.

"Gordon Cargill." Fleming suggested.

"That's the man." Jock replied firmly. He saw to it that Jessie got the same amount every month. I doubt she must have had a bank account or something for I cannae see Cargill being happy to have her coming about that fine office of his."

"Yes, that's true." Fleming said slowly. "Do you remember how much Mike left her to begin with?"

"It was eighteen thousand that came from the life insurance. That was a fortune back then and I mind o' thinking 'ye better watch yerself Mike for that bitch will kill ye for the money'."

"And the weekly amount stipulated at the time would

have been enough to subsist then but would be too little nowadays?" Fleming suggested. "There was no allowance for inflation?"

"Not that I remember. Cargill said nothing about inflation, just how long the money might last and how the interest rates would probably make the pot bigger from time to time. Mike was satisfied with that." Jock said, shrugging his shoulders. "Is it any wonder that the pair of them are living in a cave?"

"Yes, but only for the past few months have they chosen to live in a cave near to Corran Bay." Fleming thought aloud. "As far as I can tell Jessie and her boy have kept themselves nearer to Stonehouse in the past for her mother has slipped her a few quid now and again."

"That's no the way to deal wi' Jessie." Jock opined.

"It's her mother's only way of getting rid of her for a while, apparently."

"Poor old cailleach." Jock sympathised. "Imagine having Jessie for a daughter."

At this point Fleming's radio came to life and requested that he return to the office.

"I'll be back to see you again, Jock. Make sure you milk this setup for as long as you can."

The old man laughed as he watched Fleming's half-raised hand disappear out the room door.

Raymond Adam was enjoying what he saw as the winding up of the assault and rape case against Mitchell Sorbie, the Lanarkshire theft by robbery case from the sixties, the theft of poultry and the incest charges against both Sorbies. He had already begun to piece together the report that would go to the Procurator Fiscal and needed some points clarified with Fleming.

Fleming helped him as required but was unable to reflect the Detective Chief Inspector's enthusiasm.

"What's wrong with you, Andy?" Raymond Adam asked.

"I have a few nagging discrepancies." Fleming said in a serious tone.

"Nonsense. You have a lot more than fur and feathers now, surely." Adam said.

"Things may become more conclusive yet." Fleming said, still looking pensive.

"Fair enough, Andy, but we have enough and it is thanks to you, you know that."

Andrew Fleming was relieved to get away from Adam for there was no point in raising with him matters to which the Chief Inspector had given no thought and in explanation of which Fleming did not yet have answers. Matters like the inadequate income of Jessie and Mitchell Sorbie. Such circumstances were capable of providing criminal motive in people more mentally stable than the Sorbies. It was time to have a little chat with Hamish MacLeod.

"Tell me again about the Cargill sudden death, Hamish. I have read your copy report but I want to hear everything.

What was the weather like? What was Cargill doing when he died? Was anything disturbed around the place?" Fleming asked his old mate.

"It would work better for both of us if we went back out there, Andy. I don't think anything has changed. The house will be locked up but he died outside and I can show where things were." Hamish suggested.

"Yes, suppose so." Fleming said slowly. "I would prefer to ask permission from the Cargill family first, though. Hold on."

Fleming thumbed through a directory and dialled the number of the law firm, Cargill, Russell and Ridgeway. He was able to speak to Cameron Russell and explained that he and the reporting officer wished to return to the home of the late solicitor.

"The family would have no objection to that at all Mr Fleming. Is there anything wrong do you think?" Cameron Russell asked.

"No not at all Mr Russell, just looking to better understand the location by seeing it in daylight." Fleming answered, trying to make his answer sound like routine.

"Then there could be no objection from anyone." Russell promised.

Fleming and MacLeod drove out to Gordon Cargill's house and walked around it. The garden was huge but nowhere was it neglected. The plants and shrubs were past their best this late in the year but Fleming could visualise the beauty of the place with everything in bloom. They reached the French doors that led out from the study. Hamish peered through the glass after checking that the doors were locked.

"The papers are all gone now but he was working at that desk and had come out to the garden for a smoke." Hamish told Fleming.

"But nothing in the house was disturbed, before or after his death, despite the doors being wide open?" Fleming asked. Hamish had previously said that this had been the case and Fleming was reminded of that.

Andrew Fleming positioned himself at the French doors and began to walk slowly into the garden following the path of broken slabs.

"There are no lights to shine onto the garden at night, are there, Hamish?"

"Not really, Andy. The outside lamps of the house were on but they only extend to about half the distance old Cargill walked. From where you are now the path was in darkness. From there out I had to use my torch."

"And Cargill had no torch?" Fleming asked.

"I never found one." Hamish replied.

"So he walked through this trellis in total darkness to get to the fishpond and the bench seat?"

"Yes, I suppose so, but it is his garden." Hamish answered. "He could do that without seeing where he was going. Anyway, there was a moon that night."

"Okay Hamish, so he goes through this arch in the

173

trellis; would he have seen anyone hiding behind the trellis?" Fleming asked.

"Probably not but why would there be someone behind the trellis?"

"No reason yet to believe that. Cargill gets past this point anyway and reaches this circle of pathway around the fishpond. Maybe he sits on the bench seat to light his cigarette and use the cool night air to mull over whatever he was working on. He has placed his pack of cigarettes and his lighter on the armrest of the bench seat. The next thing we know he is dead and lying where?"

"He was face down in the fishpond." Hamish said.

"How did that happen?" Andy Fleming asked. "How does he get from the bench to being face down in the pond? How far into the pond was he Hamish?"

"His head was well across the pond, Andy. I reckon he had got up and walked forward to the edge of the pond when he fell forward into the pond."

"What did the post mortem have to say, Hamish?"

"It has recorded accidental drowning as the cause of death and a possible blackout of some kind beforehand. He was not a healthy bloke. He drank like a fish and smoked, obviously."

"Any indication that he was drinking that night? He was working after all. The blood reports would show any alcohol." Fleming said frankly.

Hamish was not feeling amused by this examination of his work.

"Nobody suggested that he had been drinking, Andy. As a matter of fact there are no open bottles or ashtrays in the house either."

"Did you find his cigarette end?" Fleming asked.

"No. His fag end could have gone anywhere, Andy." Hamish pleaded.

Fleming was slowly walking beyond the circled pathway, into the garden where he found it to be bounded by a low wire fence. Beyond the fence was grass and woodland forming an embankment before descending on the other side to agricultural land. Fleming walked along the wire fence looking for foot impressions but found nothing useful.

"This happened two and a half months ago, Andy. What are you hoping to find?" Hamish asked as he watched Fleming disapprovingly.

"Just anything that might be there, Hamish. Did anyone search the pond itself?"

"No, Andy. This was a sudden death for God's sake, not a murder."

Fleming wasn't really listening.

"Let's have a little rake in that water." he suggested, removing his jacket and rolling up his sleeves.

"Carry on a bhalaich." said Hamish who was not enthused by Fleming's persistence.

"Right Hamish, help me to lift this bench into the pond. If the end of it settles enough I will be able to lie on it and search the water with my arm."

"Fair enough." Hamish replied and lifted the end destined to remain on the path.

"We'll lift it from back and front, Hamish. I don't intent to walk in the water either."

The venture was successful and the far end of the bench settled down in approximately 14 inches of water. Fleming lay gingerly along the length of the bench and reached down through the murky pond until he could feel the silt beneath. With his fingers spread he searched along the supposed bodyline of the corpse as Hamish had found it. His fingers found various items that had been in the water for ages having been dropped or thrown by someone working the garden. There was nothing of any great size and nothing that could have been used as a weapon. Fleming was almost giving up on his idea when his hand met something light but metallic. He lifted it from the water to discover that it was a cycle clip. Not an old cycle clip, a cycle clip that was still good enough to stand comparison with the one in his pocket. He looked at Hamish triumphantly but Hamish just laughed.

"I see a bhalaich, Cargill got clobbered with a bicycle clip."

"No Hamish," Fleming corrected his colleague as he struggled to alight from the bench onto dry land. "He might have been clobbered by a man with a cycle clip."

Fleming showed the cycle clip to Hamish MacLeod and then took out the clip from his pocket.

"I haven't seen anyone using these things in years but

strangely enough I found this one at the scene of Karen Ratline's rape and now this one in Cargill's pond. That's a bit much of a coincidence Hamish."

MacLeod raised a conciliatory smile.

"It is a bhalaich, but you can't hope to use these against Mitchell Sorbie. How do you prove that they were his?"

"I showed this one from my pocket to Sorbie when I arrested him. We were standing at the spot where Karen Ratline was attacked but he denied a killing. His exact words were 'I never killed him'. Now do you understand why I came here, Hamish?" Fleming knew that Hamish was usually a supporter of Fleming's theories and this occasion was no different.

"You always find something that matters," Hamish said with a cheeky smile. "But you will need more to satisfy Adam, will you not?"

"In that case I will find more. Who did the post-mortem, Hamish?"

The post-mortem examination of Gordon Cargill, like all local post-mortems, had been done at the nearest general hospital, in this case Alexandria. Fleming arranged a telephone call to the pathologist named on the report, an old friend.

"Doctor Miller?" he asked hesitantly. Some pathologists preferred not to be referred to as 'doctor'. Doctor Miller had no such objection.

"Yes Mr Fleming, it is me and I have the notes from the

examination of Gordon Cargill. That is who we are going to speak about, is it not?"

"Yes indeed. The cause of death is given by yourself as 'Accidental Drowning', doctor. Did you recover much of that pond water from his lungs?"

"Actually, not that much, Andrew. That does not eliminate drowning in his case because his lungs were in a shocking state and would not require the same quantity of water as you or I. The man was in his seventies and the picture I had of him internally would not suggest an exercised or healthily attended body. I checked with his GP and found that the man had occasionally flaked out for no obvious reason. Nobody thought to stop him driving, though. He was on heart medication and the heart was not in best shape. I suspect that he simply fell forward in a condition of unconsciousness, or if not totally unconscious, then too weak to raise himself."

"How much different would the body appear to you if this man had been pushed forward into the water and held down by the back of his head, forcing his face into the silt?" Fleming asked.

"You know something, Andrew? There was silt as you call it, in his nostrils and his mouth. I put that down to his body being pulled from the pond a little ungraciously but if events followed your suggested course then I would have expected nothing different from what I found. Do you think Cargill was held down?" the pathologist asked.

"For the time being, doctor, I only need to know that it

is not out of the question. I respect your medical findings in the circumstances you were given. I just wonder for non-medical reasons if these circumstances might have been more sinister. If Mr Cargill's face had been pushed down into the silt he could have died of asphyxia without inhaling much water, agreed? I am pursuing possibilities at the moment, doctor. We shall see what develops."

"Keep me posted, Andrew."

Fleming continued with his routine duties of the day satisfied in the knowledge that Karen Ratline was coming to dinner at his house that evening. He simply had to gain her trust and get to the unspoken evidence she was keeping quiet. She was the only real witness to the attack on her at the layby and she had given a statement to the police, but she would only have responded to the questions asked. How often had he told younger officers, "Of course the witness never mentioned the answer; you never asked the question."

When he returned to the office with a handful of service executions he found Chief Inspector Stewart Mackellar waiting for him.

"You are at your bloody freelancing again, Fleming. You have taken it upon yourself to suggest that Gordon Cargill's death was not as natural as the rest of the world knows it was. What right do you think you have to probe into the post-mortem examination of a man who died almost three months ago?"

"The same right as any police officer." Fleming retaliated.

"Well I am not just any police officer, Fleming. In case you hadn't noticed, I am your Chief Inspector and I do not expect to hear from the Procurator Fiscal that you have concerns over Mr Cargill's death. I knew Gordon very well and I won't have you causing the family any more distress than they have already had. Do I make myself clear?"

"Perfectly clear, sir. Don't make waves. Just wave the flag but don't raise the standard. I've got it." Fleming said, knowing how well Mackellar would appreciate such an answer.

"And do not bother to phone your friend, Raymond Adam. I will do that for you." Mackellar said as he stormed off towards his office.

Fleming had planned to visit the offices of Cargill, Russell and Ridgeway but thought it might be more prudent to leave that until Monday.

When he reached home at the end of his working day, Fleming saw the flirting 'eyes' of Karen's mini car outside his house.

After dinner Fleming volunteered to deal with the dishes, allowing Mary and Karen to retire to the lounge. In time he joined them and patiently followed their line of conversation until Mary began to chase the children towards their baths. Now Fleming was alone with Karen and asked her how she was keeping nowadays.

"Well enough, Andy. A lot of the gap has been filled." Karen answered.

"I know that you spoke to the police at the time of your attack up the road, Karen, but I dare say there may well have been details you never mentioned. That's understandable, both then and now, but these snippets of information are often gold nuggets missed in the emotions of yourself and the officers interviewing you."

"I dare say there were some nasty little things that I never mentioned to the police." Karen said, her tone suggesting that she saw that as her right.

"That is quite natural, Karen. I must admit that I would feel like that, myself. Why should I tell them that? It is only tittle-tattle for a perverted mind."

"You are fishing are you not?" Karen asked with a slight smile on her lips.

Fleming nodded but did not smile.

"You are right, I am fishing but the untold details of your personal account would actually mean less if they came from you now. I can see a defence lawyer suggesting that words were put into your mouth by the police when they had some idea of what you might say."

"I often go over it in my mind but that is not because I want to, it's just part of dealing with it now." Karen explained.

"Yes, that is possible now, Karen, but at the time it would be an image less easy to deal with. Did you find someone in whom you could fully confide every detail, your mum perhaps?"

"Oh Lord no. Not my mother, Andy. I did speak to Doctor Wallace."

"Susan Wallace?" Andy asked.

"Yes, Susan, she was terrific. She was just the person I needed and I had never met her before." Karen said with her gratitude reflected in her expression.

"Doctor Susan would make a very good witness Karen, except she cannot disclose anything that was said between you or anything that forms part of your medical record. We both know that, but if she could speak with your consent would her testimony provide a full identifying account?" Fleming asked.

"She would be able to tell you everything that I told her?" Karen looked apprehensive.

"Yes and that could be called 'hearsay' which is not best evidence."

"Best evidence?"

"Best evidence is the evidence from the mouth of an eye witness, Karen, in this case yourself. The difficulty here is that my enquiries have progressed beyond what you have already said to the police. If you were to say something really useful in identifying your attacker now the defence would claim that the police had come to know your evidence by other means and encouraged you to corroborate their account by testifying belatedly. Do you understand?" Fleming asked.

"I think so. If Doctor Susan could repeat what I told her in confidence then it would have been my words at the appropriate time. She could confirm that I had not come to think of things belatedly as you put it?"

"Yes. I think you do understand. Do you think you could discuss this matter with your doctor, for your good health will always be her first priority and she is in a position to assess how comfortable you may have become with your memory of the nastier parts of the incident? If she says to you to 'say nothing, Karen, I don't want you going back there'. That would be good enough for me. I am not even asking at this moment for you to indicate any detail beyond what we officially know from your statement, okay?" Fleming smiled as he spoke, hoping to assure Karen of his best intentions.

"I will be going to see Susan next week, Andy. I have a follow-up appointment scheduled and we can discuss this then." Karen said, apparently content to do as Fleming had asked.

"I hope my husband found something other than police work to talk about in my absence." Mary Fleming remarked as she entered the room.

"We touched on it actually." Karen said with a smile.

The following Monday Fleming went around to the offices of Cargill, Russell and Ridgeway. He had considered taking Hamish with him but decided against it as Adam would not approve of this visit. Why place Hamish under the wrath of the Detective Chief Inspector for an idea that was Fleming's alone?

He first met Cameron Russell and informed him that he wished to know more about Gordon Cargill. Russell informed him of how the company had been formed by Gordon over thirty years before and how attached Gordon was to the local community groups and charities. He and his wife Marjorie had been heavily involved socially but with Marjorie's death five years earlier, Gordon had become more reclusive. Everyone was aware that Gordon had nothing in his life lately but his work and his social life was restricted to his office staff, those acquaintances he occasionally met in the supermarket and his housecleaner.

"If you want to know about his home life more intimately, Cathie Scott can help you. Cathie has been Gordon's secretary for the past thirty years. Nobody would know Gordon better." Russell advised.

"I will see Cathie, Mr Russell, thank you." Fleming replied. "But before I do that, can I offer you a name and you can tell me if you recognise it, Jessie Galloway."

Cameron Russell almost choked.

"Yes, I know the name. She was a client of the firm so I cannot tell you anything about her business. She was Gordon's client actually and that went back many years."

"So how do you know her Mr Russell and why the reaction?" Fleming said with a friendly smile.

"She was in here about three months back with a tall, young chap and wanted to see Gordon. I heard later that she did not like the answers Gordon had for her and the pair of them, her and the young man, had to be ushered out by Robert Ridgeway and myself. Nobody got hurt but Gordon was a bit shaken by the couple's behaviour."

"Were the police called?" Fleming asked.

"No. As I say nobody was hurt and Gordon was against calling the police. Cathie was about to do it but he stopped her. Have a word with Cathie," he offered brushing past Fleming to push open an office door. Behind a desk sat a middle aged woman with her grey hair attractively set. "I am sure that Cathie would enjoy telling you all you want to know about her old boss."

Cathie Scott's face lit up and she stood up to meet Andrew Fleming.

"I could talk about Gordon all day long Mr Fleming," she said as she extended her hand towards the officer.

"We may not have that long unfortunately, but Mr Russell has suggested that you are the authority when it comes to the personal side of Gordon Cargill."

"What do you want to know?" she asked. Cameron Russell excused himself and left them to converse.

"You can call me, Cathie. Everyone else does." the cheery secretary invited with her kindly smile.

"I want to understand Gordon Cargill, the man, in his most recent days, Cathie. Was he depressed? Was he afraid of anything? Was he under threat from someone? With regard to his work, was there a problem?" Fleming asked.

"Not really, Mr Fleming."

"Call me Andy. Everyone else does."

"Right Andy. I would not say that Gordon was depressed as much as fed-up. He was beginning to ask himself the same question that others were asking behind his back, 'why is he bothering'. Outside of this office he only ever goes home to an empty house. I have suggested that he should go away somewhere on holiday but he has taken no holidays in the last five years. He has stuck to that house of his the way he has been holding onto this office."

"How did he occupy his time at home?" Fleming asked.

"Mostly working. He would take titles home to read through or some interesting test case that he had sent for. He used his computer to study phases of history. Sometimes he would tell me about something he had explored the night before and how he had reached midnight and beyond."

"That does not sound like a man who is losing the will to live." Fleming commented.

"No, far from it." Cathie objected. "He enjoyed being at home. For him it was what he had left of Marjorie. I know how much she meant to him. When she was still alive he would ask me out occasionally in the evening to assist him to prepare larger work projects, the kind of thing he would not have considered lately. I saw enough to know that Marjorie was the social one. Gordon just wanted to please her and would accompany her for no other reason. Without her he was more reclusive and private."

"Did he drink and smoke as much as he is said to have done?" Fleming asked.

"I suppose he did." Cathie said with a smile. "He was a creature of habit our Gordon. Smoking cigarettes and drinking whisky were two of his, but he was a creature of routine too. He never smoked in the office here and he never smoked in the house at home. Marjorie wouldn't allow it and I believe he has been obeying her wishes since she died, just as faithfully as before."

"So where did he smoke?" Fleming wondered.

"Like I said, he had his routines. When he went home he made dinner and after his meal he poured his first whisky and sat down to work or study as he planned but it would not be long before he felt like a cigarette. He would always go out to the bench by the fishpond to smoke there." Cathie said with confidence. "He could be out there seven or eight times a night, even when he was working at home. He used to be a chain smoker, so Marjorie once told me"

"That would be a lot cooler out there by the fishpond." Fleming considered.

Cathie laughed.

"Oh yes, I dare say, or pouring down with rain. Gordon was not daunted by the weather. He had an umbrella by the French doors and after dinner he would be wearing his smoking jacket. It would be quite warm I imagine, it was quilted you see."

187

"So, you are saying that on the evening he died Gordon was following a normal routine of leaving his whisky indoors while he went out to the fishpond for a smoke while wearing a quilted smoking jacket?" Fleming suggested.

"I suppose so. That would be his normal. I have only been there a handful of times in the evening since Marjorie died, dealing with some more urgent work, but he did not break from the routine when I was there. I was pleased to see him using that jacket. Marjorie knew Gordon's character well when she bought it for him on their thirtieth wedding anniversary. It was either that or one of these long cigarette holders but she went for the jacket. It was a lovely colour." Cathie remembered.

"What colour was it?" Fleming asked.

"I suppose it was a pale purple really, quite a unique shade though, very smart."

Fleming said nothing but recalled the last time he had seen something purple and quilted.

"Are you all right Mr Fleming?" Cathie asked as the policeman had developed a pensive stare and had turned quiet.

"Yes, sorry, Cathie. I am just picturing the scene you are describing. Were you here when Jessie Galloway and her son caused a bit of a stir with Gordon?"

"Was that her son?" Cathie gasped. "What a big gormless bloke. Nobody knew who he was. Jessie was the client and she was Gordon's own client from years before."

She paused. "I suppose that is not strictly true, really. The real client had been her late husband. I cannot disclose that man's business but Jessie was the beneficiary of his consideration. That particular benefit was not infinite." Cathie said carefully.

"And it ran out recently." Fleming prompted.

Cathie laughed.

"You know what I am talking about?"

"Yes. I am guessing that the confrontation in the office had everything to do with the end of funding?" Fleming said with a smile.

"Oh very much so. She seemed to think that Gordon was responsible for stopping her money and she was quite nasty to him. She swore like a trooper and she stunk to high heavens." Cathie said with a disapproving look.

"Did she threaten Gordon?"

"She said she would see him in Hell for stopping his money. Gordon was quite shaken by her behaviour I thought. He never saw her as a physical threat or, at least, he never said so. The tall, quiet one could be a problem I suppose but he hadn't said anything and she never referred to him."

"Did Gordon have any other people who offered a potential threat to him?" Fleming asked. He was pleased to see Cathie consider the question before answering.

"No, not really. He had his 'opposites' socially speaking, but there is nobody who would actually want to do him harm."

189

"Thank you Cathie. You have been an immense help. This smoking jacket; do you know where Marjorie bought it?" Fleming asked.

"Oh she had to go to the city for it, Mr Fleming. It was that gent's outfitters in Gordon Street, I believe. Do you want one?" she asked cheekily.

"Don't make the mistake of thinking that I haven't shopped in there before." Fleming said with a smile. "I may yet return."

When he returned to the police office, Fleming heard that Doctor Susan Wallace had called, wishing to speak to him.

He immediately called the surgery and was connected to Doctor Susan.

"Good morning Doctor, I think you wanted to speak to me, Andrew Fleming?"

"Yes, hello Andrew. You will realise that I have seen Karen again and we spoke about her first reports to me after the attack on her. As I understand this, she did not disclose every detail to the police when she was interviewed and if she were to do so now the timing might suggest that she was simply being convenient to the evidence you have."

"I could not have put that better myself Doctor Susan. It is what you both know and did know from the outset that could provide good strong evidence, but only if we can demonstrate, as you say, that it is not simply a convenient addendum to what was said to the police interviewer. I would expect, after all that Karen had been through beforehand and the attack was still at its most traumatic, she would resist painting too fine a picture."

"You are quite right, Andrew. I had some difficulty in getting her to divulge her deeper feelings and memories. I had promised her that I would never tell anyone outside of her medical care what we spoke about. Now she has approached me to break that promise. I think that particular exercise could only be performed once, Andrew. I would also advise that Karen tell her own story in my presence. She will feel more at ease and will probably speak more freely. All we need to do is to arrange a time." the doctor told him.

Fleming was amazed at how well this idea of his was being accepted.

"You are busy, doctor, and you know Karen's hours, although she could probably be excused. Just give me your convenient time and date and I will try to accommodate it with the proper police attention. Police office or surgery?

"My office here at the surgery would suit Karen better, I think Andrew. The less formal, the better for your purposes too."

NINE

Fleming felt confident and elated as he lifted the telephone to dial Raymond Adam's number. He knew that Adam had been angry with him over the extra attention Fleming had given to a death recorded as natural and accidental. He hoped to bring the Detective Chief Inspector alongside with his latest progress.

"DCI Adam". The voice sounded rough and unsociable.

"Andrew Fleming, sir."

"What do you want Fleming? I've got two murders and an attempted murder on my hands this morning. Drug gangs at war. The third guy is in the Royal Infirmary fighting for his life. You are going to tell me that old Cargill could have been murdered too, aren't you?"

"Yes, as a matter of fact I am." Fleming said. "I have also arranged for a further interview of Karen Ratline to take place at the doctor's surgery with her doctor present."

Adam was silent for a moment, then asked.

"I'm almost sorry to ask but what is the point of that?"

"She has not told us everything." Fleming said positively. "But back when she consulted her doctor, she did tell her everything. I believe that Karen Ratline will give us far better evidence against Mitchell Sorbie on this occasion."

"But we know about Mitchell Sorbie. What can she say that we don't already know?"

"If she told us more intimate detail now then she could simply be accommodating our own evidence. She does not know that, of course, but her evidence is still her best evidence if she tells us now and her doctor, with Karen's blessing, confirms that those important details were told to the doctor long before we knew anything about Mitchell Sorbie."

Adam was silent for longer this time.

"When is this interview scheduled?" Adam asked.

Doctor Susan will get back to me on that one, sir. Both these ladies will have to be available simultaneously."

"Let me know when they are ready but remember what I said about what is going on down here. I am not exactly short of things to do." Adam said wearily.

"Right sir. I'll leave the murder of Gordon Cargill until you are ready, as well."

"Fleming, I warned you about Cargill. The man died in his own fishpond with no bugger near him. What is this about murder? What did the pathologist tell you?" Adam bellowed down the phone line.

"Doctor Miller confirmed that the cause of death could have been accomplished by a second party simply holding Cargill down in the pond by the back of his head."

"What second party? There was no bugger there." Adam roared.

"So who stole his smoking jacket?" Fleming asked glibly.

"What smoking jacket? Fleming you bas.."

Fleming hung up and walked away. It would not be too long now before Raymond Adam managed to return to Corran Bay.

In the meantime Andrew Fleming thought he would leave the office for a while. Raymond Adam was probably shouting down the line at Chief Inspector Stewart Mackellar right now and following the assault on Mackellar's eardrum; the Chief Inspector would come looking for Fleming. It was time to get some fresh air.

For Raymond Adam the day was determined to go badly. When he replaced his telephone after speaking to Mackellar, it rang again.

"DCI Adam." he announced in a slightly unwelcoming tone.

"Good afternoon, Chief Inspector, this is Cameron Russell of Cargill, Russell and Ridgeway in Corran Bay. I believe you are aware of the death of Gordon Cargill in early August?"

"I know about it, yes."

"I have a bit of a dilemma inasmuch as Midge and Donald Cargill, the daughter and son of Gordon, are heading in my direction with intentions of selling their late father's property. I understand that police interest in Gordon's death may not be entirely concluded. How free am I to act for them with regard to the property?"

Cameron Russell heard some strange breathing exercises at the other end of the line as Adam resisted any utterance and pushed his podgy hand through his less plentiful hair.

"So Andrew Fleming has been to see you, I take it." Adam asked eventually.

"Yes, he was here." said Russell.

"Has he suggested to you that Mr Cargill's death was not as natural as first thought?" Adam asked.

"I would accept that he has suggested as much. In fairness, Andrew Fleming has made no specific assertion to that effect, but I dare say he would not feel obliged to disclose the truth of the matter to me."

"I know that feeling myself, Mr Russell." Adam said, trying hard not to growl as he spoke. "I am up to my eyes in work here but I seem to have no option but to come up there and sort out our friend Fleming in one way or another. Continue to stay cool on the disposal of the property until I see you, Mr Russell. If Fleming is right, then we have to tread warily. Let me check out his mystery and I will immediately inform you of the outcome."

"Thank you very much for your patience and understanding, Chief Inspector."

"You are welcome, Mr Russell."

Adam put down the phone.

"Patience and understanding?" This time he was growling. "That'll be the day."

With the Sorbies both remanded in custody, Fleming felt free to attend to his creels and spend more time with his children. Karen or Susan would let him know of the date they had agreed upon for the interview by Adam and he had replaced the stone slab over the opening used by Mitchell Sorbie near the first crime scene. Nobody would steal the purple smoking jacket before the appropriate moment. Adam would need to arrive soon but Fleming felt sure that he would, if only to satisfy his rage.

Fleming's wife Mary was able to tell him that Karen had been talking to Jean MacIvor about taking time off work the following Tuesday to allow her to attend an interview.

The creels gave him six decent sized lobsters and almost exhausted his stock of elastic bands in one visit. As he bound the claws he wondered if the high class country hotel near his home would take them all. They did and he enjoyed handing over the cash to Mary when she came home.

Just as he imagined that his day was going really well a Ford estate car drew up outside his house. The only person he knew who drove a Ford estate car was Raymond Adam.

Because Adam had come direct to Fleming's home he showed a greater level of restraint than he felt. Even so,

Fleming knew exactly where he stood with the boss man he had hung up on earlier.

"The rape victim is not ready to speak yet." Fleming told him once the men were seated in the front lounge. "It looks like being next week, perhaps Tuesday."

"I am not here about Karen Ratline and the Sorbies." Adam said, barely concealing his exasperation. "I am here because the family of the late Gordon Cargill wish to dispose of their father's house and find that their solicitor is reluctant to act on the grounds that the police may still have an interest in the house. You are the person creating that impression and I am here to be convinced of your reasoning. This is either the serious business of murder or it is the serious personal business of your future." Raymond Adam said. "What lies behind this?"

Fleming was unperturbed. He sat back in his seat and looked Adam in the eye.

"It is at times like this that I can appreciate to some extent why some people sit on their hands more than I do." he said. "The less you do the less there is to go wrong."

Adam almost smiled.

"Cut the crap, I've heard it. I intend to go back to Cameron Russell with an answer that we can all accept. So tell me what you have to suggest that Gordon Cargill's death was murder."

"Give me a second to go to my uniform jacket, sir." I'll be right back."

Adam nodded. He expected Fleming to return with his notebook but when he came back into the lounge he placed two bicycle clips on the coffee table in front of Adam.

"Bear in mind that Mitchell Sorbie wears baggy trousers and rides a bike." Fleming said calmly. "This clip I found at the scene of Karen Ratline's rape. It was on the path there."

"And you just kept it to yourself?" Adam criticised.

"The experts had all been there so I reckoned it was of no significance to them. If I had shown it to Dougie, he would have told me that, I'm sure."

Raymond Adam scowled at him.

"Go on." he prodded.

"The second clip I found at the bottom of Gordon Cargill's fishpond."

Raymond Adam' eyes opened wide in disbelief.

"What made you look there?"

"I was actually looking for anything that had fallen into the pond along with the good Mr Cargill. There was also the chance that if someone else was involved then they could have dropped something too. In other words I searched because it seemed like the right thing to do."

Raymond Adam was open-mouthed as he considered what this cycle clip business meant.

"You have a pair of clips, how can you prove that they belong to Mitchell Sorbie?"

"I can't prove it to anyone else but let me tell you what

happened when I arrested Sorbie. I took him back through the crime scene at the lay-by and showed him the one clip that I had. I told him that I had found it and his immediate response was 'I never killed him'. I never quizzed him about that but it made me think, 'what the hell are you talking about?' You are not to know, Chief Inspector that Jessie Sorbie had been receiving a monthly payment from a trust set up by her late husband and Gordon Cargill several years ago. How else could she get by in a cave in this day and age. Poor pickings though and it is hardly surprising that Mitchell has been stealing bread and rolls from Mrs MacTaggart's shop and hens from local farms. Their needs are even more poignant now that the trust money had been exhausted and Jessie did not take that news particularly well. Cameron Russell is aware of all this and allowed me to interview Mr Cargill's secretary of many years, one Cathie Scott. Cathie had often been to the house of Cargill and had seen the late gentleman's habit of smoking at home, but only outside the house, usually beside the fishpond. When he did so, he wore a quilted, purple smoking jacket of good quality."

"Where did you find that?" Adam said, assuming that Fleming already had it.

"Let me take you to the spot where I arrested Mitchell Sorbie and we may find it." Fleming suggested.

"Why would it be there, you lifted him off the beach?" Adam asked.

"Yes, I did, and I never had the opportunity to check

out something purple that had caught my eye. It was concealed in a hole there but of course I knew nothing about the smoking jacket at that time."

Adam smiled broadly.

"And Mackellar thinks you don't understand evidence." he said, shaking his head. "All right, come with me. Better tell Mary where we are going."

Adam drove Fleming to the lay-by and the two men walked through the grass until they reached the rocks. Fleming explained how Mitchell Sorbie had been concealing himself and Fleming had climbed over the rocks looking for him. In keeping with his account, Fleming reached the top of the slab that served as a door for the hole in the rock beneath. He pushed it outwards with his foot and explained how he had fallen forward with the slab only to be set upon by Sorbie.

"We sprachled about on the ground with him trying to knock my head against the rock, the same as he did with Karen. When I got the better of him I caught sight of something purple out the corner of my eye but he was too much of a handful to take any further interest. Now we can both look at this."

Adam was already reaching into the small cave and pulling the quilted item gently from the hole. He held it up in front of him and admired the jacket.

"Terrific colour." he remarked.

"Yes sir. You obviously share your impeccable taste with Mitchell Sorbie."

Adam turned sharply.

"And the late Marjorie Cargill." Fleming added quickly.

"Have you searched this jacket?" Adam asked.

"No. You are the first to touch it since Mitchell Sorbie put it in there."

"Then let's see what these pockets hold." the Detective Chief Inspector suggested.

"Yes. Good idea." Fleming said, hoping not to sound sarcastic.

The pockets held nothing but a small business card from a local gardening firm.

"Probably been in that pocket for ages." Adam said sourly.

"Worth checking out," Fleming said more enthusiastically. "The card looks dry and crisp. Come to think of it, neither the card nor the jacket have ever been in that fishpond."

"So he wasn't wearing it." Adam said, nodding in agreement. "Better check out the hiding place while we are here."

Fleming offered to run back to his boss's car for a torch from the boot and together they peered into the small cave. Towards the back of the cave they saw a small closed knife and a white cloth. Fleming crawled into the confined space and brought both items into the daylight. The knife looked and opened like those used by fishermen and the white cloth turned out to be a pair of white panties.

"The Karen Ratline rape case has just got that bit stronger." Fleming said a little triumphantly.

"She never mentioned losing her underwear." Adam reminded Fleming.

"Perhaps she will on Tuesday." Fleming said with a smile.

Raymond Adam had lost the edge of anger that he had brought with him and now seemed more sociable, even pleasant. He agreed to take the newly found evidence with him to the police office and have it recorded there. Before doing so, he returned Fleming to his home.

Andrew Fleming's day was again showing some reward. Adam had agreed that he should submit an overtime claim for his time recalled to duty.

The following morning Fleming went to see the landscape gardener whose business card had been found in the pocket of Gordon Cargill's smoking jacket. The man could remember going to the large house around six o'clock in the evening by arrangement with the solicitor. They had discussed the garden and Cargill had given him a number of tasks to be done. The gardener had agreed to the work but would only be able to start the following week because of work already on his books.

"So did you ever start work there?" Fleming asked.

"No. I never saw him again, of course, the man died. I think it would have been that same night or maybe the following night."

"Can you check the date? It would help to be certain about that." Fleming asked him.

The contractor moved towards his office and the diary on his desk.

He looked back through the diary, telling Fleming as he did so that he had heard about Gordon Cargill's death from other customers in the days following.

"Did Mr Cargill mention to you any illness or injury he may have had at that time?"

"No. He intended to have his dinner and do some work." the gardener remembered. "Ah, here we are, Thursday 5th August at 6 p.m. Mr Cargill. 'Wants vegetable plot cleaned out and dug. Remove old plant from trellis and paint. Hedge-trimming, lawns and front beds'."

"When you were walking in the garden did either of you come across a cycle clip, the metal type that holds trouser legs tight when someone is cycling?" Fleming asked.

"I know the thing you mean. My father used to use them. No, we never found anything like that."

"What time did you leave him?" Fleming asked.

"About 6.30, we agreed on the work and the rates and then I went."

"Did you see anyone else out there, or even near there, during the time you spent?" Fleming pressed.

"No. There was nobody. Even in daylight that place is spooky quiet." the gardener said with a smile.

"You gave him your card before leaving on that evening, right?" Fleming asked again.

"Yes. That was the only time I met the man and that was when I left my card. We spoke about keeping in touch." the gardener said.

"Was he wearing anything unusual when you spoke to him?" Fleming asked.

The gardener laughed spontaneously.

"Aye. He had on this fancy purple jacket. He told me it was a smoking jacket. I asked him if he smoked and he was laughing. He said he only smoked when he was wearing that jacket."

"Did you see him put your card into the pocket of the jacket or did he do something else with it?" Fleming asked.

"No. You're right. He put the card in the pocket of his purple jacket. I remember thinking, 'if he stops smoking he'll never see that card again'."

"Sadly, you were also right." Fleming said solemnly. Gordon Cargill had died that very evening.

The day for Karen to be interviewed in the presence of her doctor was confirmed as the following Tuesday. At the school and in the police office, the interview was already an open secret. Fleming called Raymond Adam to tell him the arrangement but found that Douglas Campbell had already done so.

"I'm sorry, Andy. I know that you would have wanted to take part in this interview but I cannot allow it. It is a CID case and you were on holiday when it happened. I will be there with Douglas Campbell. It occurred to me that the Fiscal might want the interview conducted by CID officers with no prior knowledge of the case but he says 'no'. In this case the accused have too many mental health issues to expect that requirement. I hope to record the whole affair so that the Fiscal can edit out from our statements anything that would become inadmissible for any reason. Is there any question you think I should put to her?"

Fleming laughed in irony. He would have asked Karen plenty.

"I wondered for a while how Sorbie knew that a Stonehouse girl had moved to Corran Bay. It had to be her car. It is a small white mini with large Audrey Hepburn eye stickers on the bonnet. If that car sat outside her mother's house while Karen was ill then he would recognise it. He may have seen Karen before in Stonehouse; his mother certainly has and she is the instigator behind the attack. You heard her reaction to hearing that her son was being charged with rape. She hadn't ordered that, only the assault. He has a 'hands on' method of assault too. He put hands round my neck to strangle me and then chose to hold my head in order to bang it on a rock. He may have done the same with Karen and Gordon Cargill. Ask Karen if he said anything to her. I know from her earlier statement that he called her a 'Ratline bitch' but he may have said more to show the obsession his mother has ingrained in him with their covenanting past..... and don't forget the panties."

"Right Andy, thanks."

On Monday afternoon Fleming headed up to the County Hospital to see Jock but found that his friend's condition had worsened. Andy looked down on the face of a man whose complexion had shone with colour through the years. Now it was a pale grey. The lively eyes were closed. The fine white hair still looked soft and clean. The long arms and hands that lay either side of Jock's body were thin compared to their former strong muscular appearance of his working days. Jock's chest rose and fell with a gentle rhythm as it fed from the mask over the big man's nose and mouth.

"Has anyone else been to see him?" he asked the nurse.

"Yes. Mrs McPhee." she replied.

"Is he liable to wake up?" Andy asked softly.

The nurse shook her head and whispered, "I don't think so."

"How long?" Fleming asked, his expression showing the sorrow he felt.

"Not long. It may be hours or days, God will decide."

"Jock won't know about it I suppose." Fleming said. "He was a good man, woodman or not."

"He was a gentleman in here," the nurse said. "We shall miss him."

Andy wrote on a scrap of paper and handed it to the nurse.

"My home number, if you would be so kind."

Tuesday morning was bright and sunny. Fleming had received no phone call from the hospital and his thoughts were constantly of Jock, despite the knowledge of Karen's interview by Adam and Campbell. He went to visit Maggie McPhee.

"Did you get to speak to Jock before he fell into unconsciousness, Maggie?"

"Just for a few minutes, Andy. He was pretty bad. He could only talk when he felt good enough to lift his oxygen mask. He said to tell you 'goodbye'. He knew he wouldn't last. He said, 'tell him I finished his biscuits'."

Jock smiled but felt sad.

"What will happen to his caravan, Maggie?"

"He told me that I could have it, Andy. That made me cry. He had always promised it to me but I thought he was kidding. His van is better than mine. Mine can go to the dump but I wish Jock was coming back here."

"I doubt it, Maggie. He is moving up the property ladder, at least he deserves to be." Fleming said reflectively.

"Oh, I almost forgot, Andy. He gave me this to give to you. He had dug it out from an old shoebox of photos and he had it with him in the hospital."

Maggie handed Andy a small black and white photograph of two men standing in a forest of trees.

"The one on the left is Jock. Who is the other guy?"

"Michael Galloway".

The receptionist called through.

"Doctor Susan, I have Detective Chief Inspector Adam and Detective Sergeant Campbell at reception."

Doctor Susan Wallace came out to meet Raymond Adam and Douglas Campbell at the reception desk of the surgery.

"Karen is waiting in my room, gentlemen. If you would care to follow me," she said, beginning her return in that direction. "Have you both met Karen before?"

"Sergeant Campbell has but I have not spoken to Mrs Ratline before." Adam answered.

"I think she is a little uptight." the doctor said, suggesting a 'softly-softly' approach.

"She has been through an awful lot, doctor, we know that." Adam said.

"I am glad you appreciate that." Doctor Wallace said as they reached her door.

Doctor Wallace made the introductions and seated the CID officers opposite Karen who sat close to the doctor's chair.

Raymond Adam began the conversation.

"Mrs Ratline, I know that your life has been beset with circumstances that would destroy most people and now you are beginning to fight your corner very well. I know it must be daunting for you when someone like me asks you to revisit these horrible events but don't be alarmed by it. We are in possession of a lot of evidence and only wish to extract from your mind what you are comfortable to say. I believe you know Andrew Fleming?"

Karen Ratline smiled.

"Yes, we have met and he has not harassed me, if that's what you think. Mary would not allow it."

"You are right, Karen. She is closer to being his boss than I am." Raymond Adam said with a smile. "No, Andy has had the impression that your initial interview by police officers after the rape attack on you was carried out at a time much too close to the event. I can see now that he may be right. Sergeant Campbell and I are only here today to pick up any crumbs around the table, so to speak." Adam swung back in his chair and deliberately looked more relaxed. "Going back to your time in Stonehouse, your recent time in Stonehouse, staying with your mum, did you have the same little mini car that you drive now?"

"Yes. I have had that car from new, Chief Inspector. It is five years old now." Karen said easily.

"And it would sit outside your mum's house quite a lot, I imagine." Adam continued.

"All the time. I was in hospital." Karen paused to look at Doctor Wallace who gave her a reassuring nod. "The car sat outside my Mum's house all the time."

"It is quite distinctive, you agree?" Adam said with a smile.

"Everybody knows it." Karen said.

"Back in these days, Karen, we believe that Mitchell Sorbie and his mother were in the Stonehouse area. They could well have seen your car and would have known who owned it. Don't you think so?"

"His mother is the fortune-teller?" Karen suggested.

"So we have heard. Did you ever meet her?" Adam asked.

"When I was young, about fifteen, she told my fortune but she wasn't very good. She told my friend's fortune as well, but neither of us had any faith in her."

"Had you seen her since?" Adam asked.

"Yes, at least I felt sure it was her. She was outside the cemetery the day my little Callum was killed."

"Did you speak to her?"

"No, we were quite a bit apart. She kept her distance, just peered at me."

"Since then, have you seen her?" Adam asked.

"I am not sure," Karen said hesitantly. "A couple of times I thought it might have been her but that was in Corran Bay and I could not associate her with this area."

"You knew her son?" Adam asked.

"No. I never knew she had a son until my mother told me about him. She described him as weird and the folks in Stonehouse are sure it was him that attacked my friend."

"This friend was the girl Paterson, who had the Bible and groceries stolen from her?" Adam asked as if he knew the answer.

"Yes, Jennifer has seen him but just that once. His mother keeps him hidden away or at least encourages him to stay out of sight."

"Now you have seen him in much the same way as Jennifer." Adam suggested. "Brief and horrible, I dare say but did you get much of a look at him?"

"He was tall and lanky with long black greasy hair. He stunk to high heavens and his finger nails."

At this she paused and looked a touch distressed. Doctor Susan placed an arm around her shoulders.

"We think his fingernails were long, don't we, Karen?" she said softly squeezing Karen's shoulder in encouragement.

"Yes. He held my ears in his two hands and his nails dug into my ears. He was holding my ears when he was banging my head against the ground." Karen whimpered.

"The lacerations behind her ears were badly infected for a while." Doctor Susan said as she gently rubbed Karen's shoulder.

"Karen, you were raped, we all know that but I want you to think of the order of events. Were you attacked first and then sexually attacked afterwards, almost as if the rape was a second idea?" Adam asked.

Karen Ratline looked at him for a few moments before answering.

"That's right. He battered me until I was almost unconscious. My head hurt so much that I wanted to be unconscious. There was a pause, a definite pause before he did anything then I felt my clothing being removed. I realised, I realised what he was .... but then he punched me and I never knew much after that, just moments of consciousness that seemed like a nightmare."

"Did he speak at all?" Adam asked quietly.

"He was chanting."

"Chanting?" Adam repeated.

"Bunny, bunny, bunny." Karen said as if the stupidity of his chanting would deflect the shame she felt.

Adam and Campbell looked at each other in absolute surprise. They had both been present when Mitchell Sorbie had chanted that same word in the cave. On that occasion the woman had been his own mother.

"Did he ever say anything about covenanting?" Adam asked. "His mother has this obsession with the covenanters."

"No. I never heard another word, I'm sorry. I passed out. I never saw him again. An ambulance man was the first person to speak to me after that."

Adam raised a finger.

"Just one final point, Karen. You mentioned your clothing being removed. Are you missing a pair of white pants, briefs?" Adam said sounding clumsy.

"Yes. I am short of my panties but I thought it was just down to the darkness and confusion. Have you found them?"

"Yes, I think so." Adam said, turning to Campbell.

Douglas Campbell handed over a polythene bag with a label attached. Inside the bag were the white panties found by Adam and Fleming in Sorbie's hiding place.

Karen looked at them closely through the polythene and agreed that they were hers.

"Please sign the label in that case." Adam invited.

"You mentioned in your original statement that the man had a knife. Is that correct?"

"Yes, he had a knife at my throat to start with but then he must have dropped it for he was using both hands to grip my ears."

"Did you see the knife itself?" Adam asked.

"Only the blade. It was about four inches long and looked sharp but I never saw the handle."

"Fair enough, Karen. Everything you have told us today you had already told Doctor Wallace in confidence, am I right?"

"Yes. I had to confide in someone and I could never speak to my mother about such a thing."

"I understand. For the purposes of my report, Doctor Wallace, can you confirm the date or dates of your consultations and Karen's confidences of today told to you on these dates? It will obviate any claims .."

"I know, Chief Inspector. The defence cannot claim that the police tutored Karen in suitable evidence later. Andrew Fleming explained it to me pretty well."

"Of course, I am not the first to forget Mr Fleming's understanding of evidence." Adam said, aware that Campbell would later talk to Mackellar. "I thank you both for taking the time to see us today."

"Has it been worthwhile, Chief Inspector?" Doctor Wallace asked.

"In terms of evidence I believe it has, doctor. The case is stronger but." he shrugged.

213

"The chap will become a mental health prisoner?" Doctor Susan suggested. "Diminished responsibility?"

"Pretty certain." Adam said, sounding a bit disappointed, for unlike Doctor Susan, he knew of the impending murder case against Mitchell Sorbie.

Fleming's mood could not be improved by Adam' news of the interview. Nurse Mackay had called him at one o'clock that morning to let him know that Jock had passed away.

The first thing he did that Wednesday morning was to inform Maggie McPhee. The old lady was now entitled to a better caravan home but she was not for rejoicing. Fleming told her that they could attend Jock's funeral. There may not be many other mourners to attend.

Mackellar was strangely amenable to Fleming's request to attend Jock MacGregor's funeral. Dougie Campbell scoffed at the notion that Fleming should attend the funeral of such a man.

"Without that man there would be no case against Mitchell Sorbie for assaulting and raping Karen Ratline; and there would be no case against Mitchell Sorbie for murdering Gordon Cargill. Jock MacGregor was genuine. You on the other hand, puzzle me greatly."

"How so?" said Campbell with his smug grin.

"When you are busy doing nothing, Dougie, how can you tell when you are finished?"

The funeral was better attended than Fleming expected. He and Maggie were joined by Doctor Wallace, Nurse Mackay and two other nurses; Father Sullivan, a retired priest who liked to debate matters of faith with old Jock; Sam MacDonald and Tom Green, men who had worked at the power station with Jock. Also present were members of the staff at Gordon Cargill's law firm, accompanied by the son and daughter of Gordon Cargill. Word had reached them that Jock had been instrumental in bringing justice for their late boss. Word had also reached Karen Ratline, through Mary Fleming, and the young teacher turned up for the burial of a man she had never known, but by whose valuable information her attacker had been caught. Jock noticed two middle-aged men, heavily built and looking a little awkward in suits and white shirts. Their faces were those of the younger Jock MacGregor. They had to be his sons.

The Rev. Hugh MacLeod spoke at the short service of a strong and honest man who had fought his temptations over drink at one time and won the respect of all who had known him.

As 1982 drew towards its close Fleming continued to follow his own trail and joust with Campbell in matters that Mackellar insisted should be done by the CID. The winter evenings were dark and fit for nothing but the fireside and the local gossip. Mrs Paterson had made arrangements with Professor Jackson for the National Museum to act as custodians of the Covenanter's Bible.

Karen and Jennifer had made up and renewed their childhood friendship.

As the Flemings sat one evening staring at the peat fire, Mary turned to her husband and said, "Andrew, someone we know is getting engaged at Christmas."

"All right, so who would that be?"

"Karen."

Fleming sat upright in his chair.

"Karen. Who can she be thinking of marrying?"

"Apparently she has been seeing a man she met at your friend's funeral. His name is Donald Cargill."

Fleming laughed out loud.

"What's so funny, Andrew?"

"Karen could not have made a better choice. I am sure that she has finally won the full approval of covenanters everywhere."

"So Donald Cargill was a covenanter?" Mary guessed.

"He certainly was. Camilla Jackson told me all about him. He was born at Rattray, Perthshire in 1619 and executed at Edinburgh on 27th July 1681. He was a devout and respected preacher who spent most of his life on the run. I just hope the late solicitor's son can settle down and fare a bit better than his covenanting namesake did."

FUR AND FEATHERS

 The author is retired but his professional life was spent in law enforcement. An operational career in Scottish police forces was followed by roles in private health security, aviation security, civil law process and Scots Law proofing.

He is a husband, father and grandfather and now resides in Edinburgh.

GEORGE MURRAY BOOKS

Justice for Jenny and Judas

Evil Issue

Blind Love Blind Hate

The Fleming Series

The Weed Killer

Mrs Livingstone's Legacy

A Tale of Old Comrades

The Tale of the Old School Ties